The 'Chronic'les Series

The 'Chronic'les Series

Vineet Gambhir

Bigfoot Publications
Because, there's a writer in everyone.

The 'Chronic'les Series
Author : Vineet Gambhir

First Published by
Bigfoot06 Publications (OPC) Pvt. Ltd.
B-10,12 Shree Shyam Palace,
Sector 4,5 Chowk, Old Railway Road,
Gurugram, Haryana (122001)
Website: www.bigfootpublications.in
Email: info@bigfootpublications.in

First Edition : July, 2023

ISBN Print Book - **978-81-19512-19-5**

Printed in India

Dedication

To all those men and women who are, have been, or will ever be in this dilemma called "arranged marriage".

I also dedicate this to all the young women who were the true inspiration behind this book.

May you all find true love and happiness in whatever you do.

Creative liberties have been taken but with no intent to hurt anyone. Hope you enjoy reading it.

Acknowledgements

Thank you, Mom, Dad, Vijeta, Radhika, and Avirath.

No words will ever be enough to express my gratitude for your unending and unconditional love and support.

PART I

'Chronic'les of the Arranged Boy

CHAPTER 1
I BLAME THEE!

"So, do you own the entire house or just one floor in Greater Kailash?"

This was *the* very first question my could-have-been father-in-law asked me when I went to (what seemed more like an interview with him) meet his daughter, to discuss a possible matrimonial alliance.

I know they say it's not easy being an Indian girl who's turning 30 and still lives with her parents.

But believe you me, it's equally tough for a boy to be the same age and not have his wedding plans chalked out.

"Even Vineet is getting married now! And he was the most averse to the thought of getting married. If he can, why can't you?"

If only I could tell my mother that Vineet slept with enough girls to know what he didn't want from his partner and was finally settling with one who seemed to be unlike any of his previous “companions”.

I’m Abhay Mathur, and this is my story—the story of getting cornered by my parents and societal norms to get married.

“Oh, so they want you to marry someone with whom you can have sex for the rest of your life and you don’t want that. What is wrong with you?”

Well, it’s not that I didn’t want to get married or enjoy the “benefits” that come with it. I just didn’t know how to decide who to settle down with.

At the very outset, let me start by listing down everything and everyone I’d like to blame:

1. 90’s Hindi movies:

Inspired by quintessential Hindi cinema, I grew up believing in soulmates and in finding my perfect partner.

Worse still, in seeing signs when they’d come into my life, and the song and dance that follows.

But let me break that myth for you—it ain’t true! None of it is.

2. The Indian society:

The surroundings most of us have grown up in make marriage sound like it’s the most important decision of your life, and should you mess it up, there’s no going back. Of course, you can choose to part ways, but as modern as our society and families claim to have gotten, you’d still be perceived as an outcast who decided to break thy holy bond.

3. The parents:

As is the case with most Indian kids, a lot of unnecessary pressure stems from parents' urge to see their child "happily settled" as soon as they finally (after 15 long years of studying and toiling to get the best grades and jobs) start living life on their terms.

I'm sure anyone in the same situation as me would relate to this.

So in the midst of not finding my Heer (so what if I wasn't anything like Ranjha) and being surrounded by younger married cousins and least-likely-to-get-married friends, I decided to check out what the phenomenon of "arranged marriage" was all about.

CHAPTER 2
COMPREHENDING THE ARRANGEMENT

Now, before going any further, let me explain to you what a typical arranged marriage scenario looks like.

It requires two parties to begin with: the groom's family and the bride's family. It can also become a tri-party agreement in case there are relatives or matrimonial agents in the mix.

But for the sake of keeping things simple, let's keep them out for the time being.

The prospective bride and groom create eloquent one-pager write-ups about themselves, highlighting their best traits, as if to seal the deal through that tastefully written biodata alone. And please don't confuse it with your regular sexting app bio. This one has some "real" details, about your house, your previous house, your father's house, his father's house, and so on.

Now that our dear old groom is ready to be auctioned—I mean married—his biodata is circulated far and wide through all possible traditional and non-traditional channels: matrimonial websites, local priests, and newspapers, to name a few.

Once the two biodatas—please note biodatas, not the people in question—seem to match, the families decide to meet to take the discussion forward (read close the auction with the best possible bidder. And just to be clear this works both ways).

A befitting venue and a convenient day, almost always a Sunday at a hotel coffee shop nearby, are chosen for the meeting.

On the other hand, the so-called protagonists of this story—the prospective couple—go through a range of emotions at this point, from secretly and/ or visibly desperate to get married, to being passively and/ or evidently shy, and everything in between.

But this is my story, so coming back to me.

My time had come, and on one eventful day, it happened.

I was, as some would say, the "Chosen" One.

CHAPTER 3
THE "CHOSEN" ONE

It was a Sunday morning, and I was doing what most people would do after a long week of hard work—sitting in front of the TV, watching an episode of 'House of Friends' for the nth time, albeit enjoying it as much as I would have the first time I watched it.

They say the human mind is very sharp and can pick up on energies to warn you of possible dangers lurking around you.

My mind started to feel awkward, and I could sense tension filling the air. Moments later, the flag bearers who had created this energetic turbulence came into the light, cutting through the cloud of anxiety in the room.

"We need to talk, son," said my father in a heavy voice, with a mix of concern and angst on his face.

I knew exactly what that look meant. I knew it was *time*.

He continued, "We've shortlisted a few girls for you. They all seem like fine young women. Have a look and tell us when we can start meeting them," while handing over a bundle of printouts to me.

A sudden silence fell upon us. Everyone was figuring out what to say next, including me.

Just then, my mother abruptly broke the calmness. She had more important things to add.

"Vivek is also getting married next month. Rohit is younger than you, and he got married last year. Time is running out. There won't be a better time than now. You *must* be ready to start meeting girls. It took your sister two years to finally find her husband. Who knows how long it may take for you? You are anyway very picky. But look at us. Haven't we made it work for so many years? Now's the time, son. You can do it. You must do it. You have to do it," she gasped.

As I said, growing up on cheesy romantic movies made me want to find someone I could fall in love with. Someone I could woo and dance around trees with, and finally get married to. But as I was growing up, that dream of finding my princess started to blur. And during this conversation, more so than ever, it seemed to be just that—a dream—that I probably needed to wake up from.

So I thought it was best to stay mum, go with the flow and see where this adventure takes me.

It's not that I wasn't thrilled about the idea of meeting someone *just* once or twice before deciding to marry them. But I honestly hadn't been with someone for a while and couldn't think of a reason to dismiss the possibility of meeting someone through this arranged setup.

"Sure, let me go through these profiles and get back to you."

My parents couldn't contain their excitement. It was as if they were already visualizing the entire wedding playing out right in front of their eyes. And seeing the sparkle in their eyes, my decision to meet and settle down with a stranger whom I'd met just once or twice, became even stronger.

After a careful screening process of matching horoscopes and the marriage-friendly version of "ASL?", we identified a girl whom I was to meet.

CHAPTER 4

THE CRORE-PATI ONE

The venue chosen was a premium hotel in South Delhi.

We arrived a little before the other family and settled ourselves on a comfortable lounger in the coffee shop just ahead of the lobby.

My parents and I chose a table that had a clear view of the hotel entrance and sat on one side of it.

But we were not prepared for what came next.

Moments later, we saw what looked like a shiny new SUV halt right in front of the hotel gate, and the family that emerged from it was just as big as their ride.

The girl in question hopped off the car first (I'd seen her photograph so recognized her instantly), with her parents behind her.

They were followed by two girls who looked a lot like her, a guy who looked nothing like any of them, and an uncle who was visibly out of place.

Her father scanned the coffee shop and identified his target (me!), and they all came running towards our table.

Mr. Kapoor introduced himself, his wife, and their younger daughter, Pooja, whom we were here to meet.

He then pointed to their elder daughter and her husband.

Apparently, the sisters were inseparable and made all decisions together.

Then to Pooja's maternal uncle who had always been a well-wisher of the family, and lastly to Pooja's best friend who'd also accompanied them. Because why not?

We exchanged pleasantries and got seated, just as my prospective father-in-law (pFIL going forward) broke the awkward silence by shouting out to the waiter and motioning him towards our table.

We ordered some tea and snacks while setting the stage for the weirdest conversation of my life.

"So, do you own the entire house or just one floor in Greater Kailash?" my pFIL asked my dad.

"We own one floor. It's a spacious 3-bedroom house," my dad replied.

"Oh, *ji*! Very lovely. Ours is a 3-story mansion in Panchsheel Park with an open terrace. Goddess Laxmi has been so kind to us always that we've got more than what we need. I can't tell you, our future son-in-law will be the luckiest man on the planet," he laughed.

Everyone just smiled, as this was too much to take in within the first 120 seconds of our *first-ever* interaction.

"So, have you always been in Del..." My father had barely finished his question when pFIL jumped in to say, "We've always been in Delhi. We own a 2-acre farmhouse in Chattarpur, as well as a *small* 5 BHK house in East of Kailash, apart from the mansion we live in now. Our future son-in-law will be the luckiest man on the planet."

"I believe your son is a Marketing Manager. How much does he earn?" Pooja's mother asked in a genuinely curious tone.

I wasn't sure if I were to answer this question directly, but I didn't want my parents to make small talk either, so I just replied, "25 lakhs per annum, Aunty".

"That's nice!" shouted her sister. "But Pooja can shop for that much in one month alone."

Everyone in her family laughed.

No one in mine did.

It wasn't so much about their bragging, but I was starting to get annoyed by the fact that no one seemed interested in getting to know the real me or my aspirations.

Worst of all, Pooja hadn't even spoken yet, and with the sheer number of people at that table and the decibel level at which they were speaking, I doubted her turn would ever come.

Yes, she was a pretty girl and had I met someone like her at a bar, I would have been desperate to get her number. But her family's attitude was such a turn-off that I felt like inverting the freshly served hot cups of tea on their heads, one by one.

I've always been taught to give people the benefit of the doubt. So I thought I'd wait it out just a little longer to see what they were actually all about.

"We went for our honeymoon to Europe for 2 weeks. The business class travel was just a whole new experience. Wasn't it, baby?"

I wanted to punch Pooja's brother-in-law when he said that.

He wasn't rude or anything, but I just felt that hitting him at that moment would bring me a lot of joy.

I obviously decided against it.

After gathering all the necessary details about my bank balance, movable and immovable assets, fixed deposits, and investments, my pFIL suggested that the girl and boy should catch up for some time, alone.

And by "alone" he meant sitting two tables away and having the same awkward conversation, one on one.

I wasn't keen on going ahead, so I looked at my parents, hoping for a sign in return to help me avoid going through with this.

And then suddenly, Pooja's BFF shouted in the shrillest voice I had heard in my entire life, "I'll go sit with them too."

That was the final straw for me. It was *just* the sign I was looking for.

I looked at my parents again, and this time they shook their heads. I knew we were on the same page.

"It has been lovely meeting you, Mr. Kapoor. Let us all think this through, and we can connect again in a few days," said my father, gesturing to the waiter for the bill.

We cleared the bill, got up, and politely stepped out of the coffee shop.

I saw Mr. Kapoor and their entire family looking both shocked and confused. They couldn't believe that someone would not be interested in their "million-dollar daughter".

I could almost see him mouthing the words, "Our future son-in-law will be the luckiest man on the planet."

But I couldn't care less, and all I felt was unprecedented respect for my parents as we walked out of the hotel gate.

CHAPTER 5
THE HOT SEAT ONE

The first meeting taught us a few things, and I knew I had to be better prepared the next time.

That said, I'd also been told at the beginning that patience is the key to finding the right life partner, and I shouldn't give up hope too quickly.

So this time, I did the research myself. I went through multiple profiles, understood the family background, and shortlisted a profile that (I felt) fit best with mine.

This was a family of three, all of them architects, based in Kailash Colony.

The girl in question, Ashima, had been a scholar throughout, completed her Master's in the UK, and was working with her father in their own firm in Gurgaon.

And I won't lie to you, she was by far one of the prettiest girls I had ever seen. One look at her photograph and my faith in the concept of arranged marriages was instantly restored.

We met at another hotel's coffee shop, also in South Delhi.

They had arrived a few minutes before us, and I was already impressed.

I was searching for Ashima when I realized she had gone to the washroom. Just as we were seated, I saw her emerge from behind a large, ornate centerpiece placed on our table.

She was beautiful in the most conventional sense—large hazel-brown eyes, a peaches-and-cream complexion, waist-long dark brown hair, and she was wearing a baby pink Indian dress.

I couldn't take my eyes off her, and that's also (read mainly) why I wanted this meeting to go perfectly.

It started on a great note as Ashima's father, Mr. Khanna, spoke about their family traditions, strong values, and the fact that he had worked diligently to provide a comfortable life to his family.

Ashima, too, was a great conversationalist. She seemed like a vibrant, fun girl, talking passionately about her vocation and hobbies, while I listened to her, mesmerized.

She talked about her love for movies and then suddenly looked at me and said, "I hope you like RJK too. Because I just loooove him!".

Being an ardent Hindi cinema admirer myself, I understood she was talking about Rajveer Khan. But with the range of emotions I was experiencing at the time, I just smiled and nodded gently.

Then came the time for the "children" to sit together and talk, and I would be lying if I said I wasn't looking forward to it.

She was such a happy-go-lucky, positive girl, with the exuberance of a little child!

I wanted to come across as the perfect gentleman, so I asked her to walk in front of me, pulled her chair, and even asked if she was comfortable, once she was seated.

Now, it was time for me to just fall in love with the woman of my dreams.

A couple of minutes into the conversation, she asked me enthusiastically if I liked celebrity chat shows. In an attempt to match her energy, I nodded vigorously.

Meanwhile, she reached into her unicorn-embossed purse and took out a bundle of sheets that had been clipped together with a unicorn clip.

"Let's play rapid-fire now! I'm going to ask you some questions, and you have to answer with the first word that comes to your mind."

I wasn't sure if she was joking or serious, but she wouldn't have said all that if she wasn't.

"It's going to be a super fun way for us to get to know each other. So let's dive straight in!"

Before I knew it, I was in the game, both literally and figuratively.

"Favourite colour?"

"Umm...sorry?"

"Just answer, what's your favourite colour?"

"I guess blue."

"Favourite movie?"

"Can't think of one. There are quite a few."

"No, but we need one!"

"Okay, maybe 'Chronic'les of the Arranged Boy."

"Favourite TV show?"

"That's easy, House of Friends!"

"Favourite pizza topping?"

"Chicken Salami and Feta Cheese."

"Your best feature?"

"I'd say my smile."

"Your best quality?"

"Patience."

Sitting and answering her questions clearly required a lot of patience, I thought to myself.

"Now, choices, very quickly. Mom or Dad?"

"Umm, Mom."

"90's Indipop or contemporary?"

"90's music any day."

"Chocolate or Strawberry?"

I know she wasn't talking about condoms here, although I so wish she was.

"Chocolate."

"Skating or Swimming?"

"Swimming."

"Slime or Plasticine?"

"Slime?"

"Great. Now rate these in order of preference. Career, Love, Family, and Friends"

"Are you serious?"

"It's fun, no? Just do it!"

"Okay, Family, Career, Friends, Love."

Remember how I said, she seemed like a happy-go-lucky, positive girl with the exuberance of a little child?

Well, she was exactly that—an over-energetic, boisterous little child!

One whom I wasn't interested in fathering.

Before she could say anything else or take out another game from her unicorn purse, I knew I had to get up and leave.

With not much more to lose, I thought I'd turn on my tongue-in-cheek humour as well.

"This was great. I hope I'm getting my goody bag now." She giggled like a schoolgirl, as I began to rise from my seat.

“Don’t you want to know my answers to the same questions?” she exclaimed. “Believe me, I’m going to be super rapid and fiery”.

I felt like I had lost an entire day and was also quite frankly tired after this impromptu gaming session. Playtime was over, and I felt I needed to be around people twice my age to balance out the last hour I had spent.

The meeting had come to an end, and I felt a strange emptiness inside me. My mind was filled with questions of if, when, and how.

But as they say, the third time’s a charm, so I was ready to give this one more shot.

CHAPTER 6
THE BTM ONE

Being a fairly analytical guy, I started analyzing the trend to see what could have led to my disastrous meetings.

After careful scrutiny of all the facts and figures in the profiles I'd seen so far and the girls I'd met, I came to a conclusion.

It was right in front of my eyes, but I couldn't believe I hadn't seen it.

There was one thing common to these girls - South Delhi.

I realized it was time to broaden my horizon, quite literally. So, I decided to meet girls from a much larger area now - Delhi.

Don't judge me. That's almost four times as big, and hence four times as many women too.

So, after going through a couple of hundred profiles, I found one that seemed very suitable.

This time, I went the extra mile to ensure things went right, so I started by finding someone who, among other things, also shared my zodiac sign.

Kriti Tandon was also a Cancerian like me, and I knew our kind were overly sensitive, fiercely loyal, and largely reserved.

She had a master's in biology and was a high school teacher in a reputed school in Delhi.

And finally, the best part, she wasn't from South Delhi, but Pitampura instead.

With all of this in place, I knew nothing could go wrong this time.

We met at a hotel in Connaught Place since it was convenient for both families. Kriti's family was already there, and they greeted us with warm, genuine smiles.

In no time, our families were talking as if they had known each other for years.

Kriti didn't speak much, and it seemed like it was one of her first such meetings. I remembered how my first meeting had been, so I could totally empathize with her.

She seemed visibly awkward and out of place, but she had a very genuine smile with dimples on both sides.

I could feel fireworks inside me every time she smiled. Could this be the start of my perfect love story?

"It's a great profession to be in. But no one in your family is a teacher, so how did you get interested in it?" my mother asked Kriti.

Her eyes suddenly lit up as if she had been waiting for someone to ask this question. She raised her head gently and started talking about her subject.

It was heartening to see the passion in her eyes as she spoke about the magnificence and science of the human body and how it works.

The moment came for the two of us to spend some time alone, and I almost blushed at the way she looked at me from the corner of her eye.

She was so shy and uncomfortable that I felt it was my duty - being a 'senior' in the marriage department by exactly two meetings - to make her feel at *home* (so she'd want to come to mine).

"Shall we sit there?" she asked, pointing towards a table that was at the end of the coffee shop. She almost whispered so I could barely hear her.

"Sure," I said loudly. My excitement was evident.

We walked to the table, and she sat with her back towards the table where our families were.

"Can my father see me from here?" she asked softly once we were seated.

"No, not really. Why?"

"Aah! I can't begin to tell you, dude. *This* has been such a nightmare," suddenly the pitch in her voice increased significantly. She was no longer whispering, and I could see her talking with a lot more confidence and ease.

"Umm, what has?"

"I made the mistake of telling my parents about Abbas. I was so in love with him, but my parents like rejected him just because he was from a different caste."

My throat choked, and I could barely get words out of my mouth.

"Oh. So do you want to marry him then?" This time, I spoke in whispers.

"No, no. That chapter's over now. It was difficult to get over him, but I like learnt from that and didn't make the same mistake again."

"That's good to know."

"Yeah, totes dude. That's why the next guy I was with wasn't from a different caste. But Dad didn't like Karan either because he wasn't as rich as us. I mean, can you believe it?"

"Yeah, unbelievable," I said.

Although this was just *one* of the many unbelievable things that my mind was processing at the time.

"I'm so happy that you're being so honest about all these things."

"Yeah, dude. It's all about being super honest. I'm like, 'Dad, give me a break.' He hasn't approved of even one guy I've been with. I kid you not, not ONE."

And *I* kid you not, two waiters and a few people turned in our direction when she shouted, “One”.

“Wow! Sometimes parents can be so unreasonable,” I said. I hoped she could sense my sarcasm.

“I know, dude, especially for Karan. I mean, he was absolutely delicious.”

I was overwhelmed with all the information that had come my way. But I decided to clear my head and continue the conversation.

“If you don’t mind me saying, you seem to have been with a lot of guys.”

“Weeeelllllll, about a dozen, give or take. And, and, I believe there’s going to be an addition to that list very soon,” she said winking at me.

I let all of this sink in. I couldn’t believe that the same girl who had trouble getting words out a few minutes ago was now saying all this to me.

But I had to understand what was going on, so I gathered my thoughts yet again and asked her why she was planning to get married, and if this is how she wanted it.

“Dude, don’t get me wrong. I’m, like, a very giving person. I love myself, and I love everybody around me. I’ve explored enough, and now I want to give all of this love out to my husband.”

She paused for a few seconds and said, “Do you want to like experience some of it?”

My face dropped.

Yes, a few hormones started churning inside me, but that was just for me to know.

She could only see my confused, expressionless face.

"You don't mean that do you?" I asked.

"Of course, dude. We can totally sneak out for like a couple of minutes."

"How? I mean it's..."

"We can say we're going for a walk. Come on, don't be a wuss. Don't you want to know your to-be wife better? I know I want to *open* up to you," she winked again.

I didn't know what to do - I was torn between my integrity and what my raging hormones were asking me to do.

She started to graze her hand against my thigh, and I suddenly got up.

She probably thought I was going to the washroom, and she was supposed to follow. But instead, I walked up to our table and told my parents we had to leave.

Moments later, we were on our way back home, and all the way I kept thinking if I had made the right choice.

After all, she probably was the hottest girl ever who wanted to make out with me. But I knew I was a righteous man, brought up with good values and beliefs. I did what was morally and ethically right.

Okay, fine! Who am I kidding? I was, in her words, "like a totes wuss, dude" for saying no. I knew I was going to regret this for the rest of my life.

Oh well, it was time to leave the guilt behind and move on.

But where to now?

CHAPTER 7
THE 6-9-18 ONE

I told my parents that I would find someone on dating apps or remain single for the rest of my life because going and meeting people like this had started taking a toll on me.

But then again, a man has needs, doesn't he?

So when you clear your mind of doubts and start focusing on what you truly desire, the mind gives you new ideas and perspectives that take you straight to your goal.

The same thing happened to me as well. After my last setback, I decided to give this whole marriage chapter a break.

And that's when it dawned on me - I didn't necessarily have to *meet* my prospective brides!

I could just get to know them better the old-school way - through messages and calls. And if things worked out, the families could meet then.

Eureka! I felt like my IQ was higher than 160 at this point. After basking in the glory of my idea, I decided to find the next young lady I had to speak to, quite literally.

Ramya Rathore was a digital marketer who was born and brought up in Bangalore (read not Delhi) and was living with two flatmates in Gurgaon.

Before speaking to her, I decided to check her social media profile to be doubly sure. Because who you are on social media is how you are in reality as well, right?

After spending a few hours examining her profile, I concluded that she seemed like a fun, progressive girl who had so much in common with me.

My excitement level was up again, and with stars glistening in my eyes, I started hoping this was it.

I texted her on the number in her biodata and waited for her reply. She replied after a couple of hours, and we started chatting.

I introduced myself and spoke to her about why I had messaged. To be honest, she didn't seem very excited. But I figured that could be because she was speaking to a stranger, that too for the possibility of getting married. It was supposed to be awkward.

Before you ask, I had become pretty thick-skinned by now. I didn't feel the butterflies in my stomach anymore.

Although, I'm not sure if that was a good thing.

Anyway, since we had a lot in common, it wasn't difficult to initiate a conversation. We spoke about movies, sports, the latest trends in digital marketing, and of course, the thread that brought us together - marriage.

But there was something that kept bothering me. Even after a couple of conversations, I realized she wasn't very comfortable discussing the topic of marriage or the slightest possibility of us getting together.

Perhaps that's why this had become some sort of forbidden fruit that my heart was yearning for dearly. Through our conversations, I had grown fond of her and hence didn't want to let this go without a fight.

So one (not so fine) day, I decided to confront her.

"We've been speaking for a couple of weeks now, Ramya. It's been good so far and I really like talking to you."

"Abhay, please stop right there," she said.

"What happened? I mean, didn't we know we would have had to discuss a possible future together, at some point?"

"I know, but I don't think this would work out."

I felt pretty bad hearing that because in my head it had been going pretty well.

"Of course, it's your call at the end of the day. And honestly, I've been getting that vibe too. But I don't understand why. Is it something about me?"

"No, it's not that. It's complicated. I don't know how to tell you."

"Is there someone else? Let's be straight with each other and address the elephant in the room."

"Well...I don't know if I'm doing the right thing by telling you this, but you seem like a nice guy so here goes."

"It is not so much in the *room* as it is in the closet."

"What do you mean?"

"You are right that there is someone else in my life. Jaspreet, my flatmate, well...*she* is not just my flatmate."

"Wait. She's a she?"

"Yes. We're madly in love, and my parents will never understand this. You wanted me to be 'straight' with you. But well, that's the irony," she laughed.

As you've witnessed, throughout this journey of meeting and speaking to different women I've been shocked many a time. But this one took the cake, the baker, and the bakery too.

"Oh wow, so what next?"

"I don't know. We'll just have to run away maybe. Although I don't care because the government is with us now."

She continued, "You know on 6-9-2018, Section 377 was dismissed and so Jaspreet and I don't have to live in fear anymore. We're going to be together, and if my parents don't allow that, I'm just going to live with her like we do now."

I didn't know whether to feel bad for her or to thank my dear stars for making me go through this experience as well.

Like I hadn't seen enough?

"Wow, I did not see that coming. But all I can say is that you're doing the right thing by following your heart and I wish you guys…umm, girls…a lot of happiness together."

"Thanks, Abhay. You're a really nice guy. Good luck with your search."

Man, this was not getting any easier. I really thought I should write a book about my experiences!

A lot of people in the same situation would understand my plight, and relate to this supremely unnerving rollercoaster ride.

Oh, that rhymed!

CHAPTER 8
THE ILLUMINATED ONE

By now, I was sure that I was destined to remain single for the rest of my life. I was certain that the institution called marriage was not for me.

I knew God had played a huge prank on me, and my entire life was a big fat joke. In other words, all hope was lost.

Or was it?

It was a lazy Sunday afternoon, and something totally unexpected happened.

You might recall that all the women I'd met or spoken to so far had been identified and shortlisted by me and my family.

But something different happened this time around.

Around 3:00 PM, my father got a call from a certain Mr. Suri.

He wasn't just anybody. He was *the* Mr. Suri, B.A., L.L.B. - an extremely reputed lawyer who was in the news every other week (that too for the right reasons). He had a successful, flourishing business in Gurgaon, with a lot of residential and commercial properties all across the country and even outside.

While we were happy to know that he had called asking for me, I was curious to know why such a celebrated man would want me for his only daughter.

He addressed my query himself by telling us that he had heard really good things about me and the family from a common, trustworthy friend and that all he was looking for was “a well-brought-up boy”.

It seemed both exciting and reassuring at the same time.

To be honest, I was happy, for my confidence had just got a much-needed boost.

We got to know from the same common friend that the girl in question was also very cultured and spiritual, and hence I would be “lucky” to find a match like her.

While I wasn’t too hopeful about this alliance, people around me made me believe that I’d lucked out and had to give this a shot. And although I’d had a string of pretty crappy experiences, I didn’t want this one to be one too.

So I decided to do things differently this time as well - I proposed meeting her alone first. It seemed best to know each other one-on-one, without any parental pressure or fear of judgement.

To my surprise, her family agreed, and we decided to meet at a posh restaurant near her house for an early dinner at 6:00 PM.

The restaurant was my favorite spot in town, so I was sure that at least the food would not let me down, even if the meeting did.

And then she entered.

I kid you not, I could smell her perfume from where I was sitting. It was a seductive mix of wild berries and peppermint.

Before I could make sense of what was happening, I saw her standing right in front of me with her hands folded.

I quickly got up from my chair and reciprocated the greeting.

"What impressive Indian values," I thought to myself.

I'd heard that she was tall, but she was like 6 feet. I had never seen a woman as tall as her.

She had the most beautiful, dusky complexion, majestic grey-green eyes, and shiny, poker-straight hair.

"Hi Radha, how are you?"

"I am doing well Abhay. I sincerely hope you are too."

She had the most sultry yet serene voice I had ever heard.

Ooh, how did I get so lucky?!

"Could you pardon me for my delay, please?" she said in the most calming way.

"Sure, that's not a problem. I just got here some minutes ago."

"A few."

"I'm sorry?"

"*A few* minutes ago. Some minutes ago would be incorrect as 'some' is for uncountable things."

"Oh! Uhhh, yeah. Alright."

"I'm sorry, I hope you didn't feel I was putting you under a scanner. I have this innate need to correct people's grammar."

It was as if my high school English teacher had disguised herself as a seductress and come to meet me. (Thankfully) she didn't look anything like my teacher - just an extremely attractive creation of the Almighty, with the voice of a siren.

We got talking, and she started discussing things, right from life after death to karmic blueprints.

A few minutes into the conversation, I felt like I was in a Yoga Ashram, being tutored on therapeutic life experiences.

"You have a very genuine smile, Abhay."

"Thanks, that's very kind of you."

"A day without joy, laughter, and smile is a day that's just not worthwhile."

I was quiet. So was she.

She seemed at peace. I, on the other hand, had questions.

"You're really into spirituality, I've been told."

"Being spiritual is a virtue that's overrated, but I would strongly recommend it to the uninitiated."

"Uhh, that's enlightening."

"Enlightenment is just a state of mind. Everyone can experience it when they look beyond the grind."

Was it just me, or did everything she say sound like it rhymed?

"Wow, that's beautiful."

"Beauty is temporary and lies in the eye of the beholder. It's your compliment that will stay with me, even when I'm older."

I'd casually asked her if she was spiritual, but by doing so, I accidentally unleashed a side of her that was overtly lyrical. Oh, I can rhyme too!

But I knew I had to bring the conversation back to why we were meeting. Although, I wanted to have a little fun of my own as well.

"So, who, in your opinion is the right partner for you?" I asked.

"Well, no one is right or wrong. They're just different, and you need to embrace them in every shape, size, or form."

"That's deeply profound." I wanted to project myself as a higher being, so I started using fancy words myself.

"But who do you know is the perfect person for *you*?"

"We know perfection does not exist, so finding that perfect person is something you should resist."

So, by that logic, you should just marry the first person you meet. I so wanted to say this to her face, but for obvious reasons, I kept my sarcasm to myself.

"That's great. I agree with that wholeheartedly."

"And what does the institution of marriage mean to you?" I asked.

"Marriage is an alliance of two bodies, minds, and souls. An institution of patience and compromise in which one enrolls."

"However," she continued, "if you're willing to work on it and lower your guards, it promises you great rewards."

By now, I was happy about my choice of venue. The delectable food was definitely lifting my mood. The conversation, too, was surprisingly amusing to me. I wasn't irritated or angry. Had I grown up?

Although, I almost felt guilty for not having paid for this class of enlightenment by this priestess who continued to shower me with her pearls of wisdom.

I was, in equal parts, both intrigued and amused. But I knew it was time to wrap this up with a few final questions.

"What plans for the future then, Radha, and where do you see your potential partner fitting in?"

"The purpose of my life is to be peaceful, gratified, and content. And as for my life partner, I'll read out a beautiful message my Guruji sent."

She continued, "The message is inclined spiritually, so I sincerely hope you can follow me."

Oh boy, could it *be* any more spiritual?

"Love is merely a four-letter word - Lavish, Odd, Vivacious, and Errored. The kindred spirit with whom I'm meant to be…will call out to my soul wherever I am and come to me."

I almost got up from my seat to felicitate her with a slow clap. But I didn't.

With utmost certainty, I knew we would never meet again. And so I wanted to have one last laugh.

I was convinced that I owed this much to myself, after having gone through what I had in the last few months.

So I quickly took out my phone from my pocket and searched the internet for a deep, meaningful farewell limerick.

I cleared my throat and said, "The time has come to bid farewell, with that, I wish you the best and hope you always excel."

Her eyes widened, and for the first time, I saw discomfort in her otherwise calm and poised demeanour. Although it was just for a few moments, it brought me eternal joy and solace.

We split the bill, courteously bid adieu to each other, and went on our separate ways.

CHAPTER 9

CHECKING OFF THE CHECKLIST

She has to be pretty!

She has to have a sense of humour!

She has to be well-read!

She has to love my parents as much as I do.

She has to have the same life goals as me!

Well, I started out looking for that perfect girl. But on the way, I realized there is nothing like perfection.

I mean, to begin with, I know I'm not perfect. So expecting someone else to be was wrong, to say the least.

Maybe it's not about finding the "perfect" girl after all. It's about finding the perfect girl *for me*.

Then again, who would qualify as my perfect life partner?

Is it someone who's exactly like me? Someone who would inherently know what makes me happy and what riles me up. Or is it someone who's just the opposite? Someone who would complement me perfectly and make up for my shortcomings.

So let's go over the list again.

She has to be pretty.

Does she?

She has to have a sense of humour.

Does she?

She has to be well-read.

Does she?

She has to love my parents as much as I do.

Does she?

She has to have the same life goals as me.

Does she?

Yes, I know what you're thinking - no, she does *not*!

After going through these experiences, I realized it's not about sticking to a checklist.

It never was!

It's also not about the arranged versus the love marriage setup.

There are umpteen examples of both working extremely well and otherwise.

It's really about finding 'that' someone who just clicks. It's not something that's easily understood, because it's a voice that comes from deep within.

Of course, the voices of your "well-wishers" just make it harder to listen to this inner calling.

And then there is your own checklist - things that you've always thought to be true. Perceptions and ideas that have simmered in your mind for long and have become your belief system. Notions that have clouded your judgement and thoughts in a manner one can't even fathom.

So what do you do? Well, let me share some nuggets from my personal experience. Here goes.

Step 1:

My sincere advice to anyone in this situation is to write down your checklist on a piece of paper. Write down everything you've heard, believed, and been told would be the qualities of an ideal partner.

Next, take a good look at that list, pick up that paper, and tear it up real nice. Yes, you read that right.

You're looking for a person, not going grocery shopping. You just *have* to throw away your checklist, literally and figuratively.

Is that all? It can't be that simple, eh?

You're right. There's another thing you must do.

Step 2:

Shut out every voice around you and in your head, so you can listen to your inner self clearly.

No, I'm not hungover from my last meeting with the demi-goddess to be saying all of this. I genuinely feel that there are way too many rules and guidelines that are fed to us right from our childhood.

On top of that, there are cultural norms, things you learn from books and movies. Not to forget the unending comparisons you or your family make with friends, neighbours, and cousins.

And in all this noise gets drowned, the voice that tells you who's the right partner for you.

It's not about going by a book, and most definitely not going by what others want in your life partner. It's about knowing yourself well. Go inward because you know who you truly are – your hidden desires and expectations, your innermost strengths, and your weaknesses.

There's no room for pretence there, just the actual, real, naked *you*! And only after you've really understood what you desire, it'll be time to meet and know people. Only then can you truly understand who they are and give them that comfort and space for them to also be their most authentic self.

Final Step Alert - Step 3!

And you're done. All you need to do now is let your head and heart guide you to the right person.

You'll know exactly if this is the person who'd be a contribution to your life and more importantly, vice versa.

There are going to be imperfections, there are going to be challenging times, and there are going to be bouts of doubt.

But well, that's what life is also about, right?

You find workarounds instead of complaining. You learn to embrace differences rather than blaming (yourself or them).

You understand everyone is human and bound to make mistakes, and that they're going to make this relationship work with the same intensity and intent that you would. So just clear your head, follow your heart, and take the plunge.

How do I know all this, you ask?

Well, I can tell you because I did end up finding my "one".

Yes, it happened.

And that too in the most mysterious of ways.

It turned out to be a pretty interesting experience and totally worth it. But that's a story for another day. Hope to see you on the other side.

Until we meet again, stay sane, and may you most definitely find your *one*.

Adios!

<Insert cheesy, emotional line here.>

CHECKLIST

Make a list of everything you've wanted in your life partner…

…and cross it out!

PART II

'CHRONIC'LES OF THE MARRIED BOY

CHAPTER 1
"I AM"

"I am strong."

"I am confident."

"I believe in myself."

"I love myself."

"I am complete even by myself."

This was my morning ritual for over a month. I would repeat these affirmations in my head every morning to recover from the 'trauma' I had gone through last year.

If you've forgotten, let me recap it for you - I'm Abhay Mathur - the guy who (in)famously went looking for his soulmate through the arranged marriage process only to be disappointed every step of the way.

Someone who was a true believer in old-school romance had given up on the very idea of falling in love.

What's worse is that he had given up on something even more precious - himself.

But Abhay was not a quitter. Being a true Cancerian, he had deep emotions but also a strong crab-like exterior. It was time to channel some of this external strength and bring back his innate confidence and self-love.

Wait, isn't this my story? Why am I talking in the third person?

Okay, coming back.

Irrespective of *my* relationship status, I knew there was one relationship in my life that I couldn't afford to give up on - the one with myself. So I started looking for ways to remind myself how amazingly blessed I was.

It wasn't easy and most definitely not very quick either. But a combination of working out, daily affirmations, and good food did the trick. No, I wasn't in rehab, although my routine does sound like one.

In about a month's time, I was back to being my usual happy self. Or maybe an even better version of myself since I had risen from (what felt like) ashes.

The phoenix was back, ladies and gentlemen.

Presenting Abhay 2.0!

New and improved, now with extra self-confidence.

Oftentimes in life, things happen to you when you least expect them. I feel the more desperate you are for something, the more it evades you.

So, I decided not to think about my love life anymore, at least for the time being.

CHAPTER 2
DEFINITELY NOT HER

With (a lot) more time at hand and an even clearer focus on the most important things in life, I was not only doubly efficient at my job but also a much happier person.

I immersed myself in work and went above and beyond my core duties. The impact I made became so evident that it was impossible for anyone to not take notice. I was receiving all the adoration from my bosses and colleagues. I even started proactively taking on bigger projects just to keep myself productively occupied.

Even outside of work, I started socializing like never before.

I attended every event, dinner, and party that I was invited to (even a few that I wasn't invited to).

I would eagerly wait for an invitation and probably be the first person to RSVP. The idea was to keep my mind off the four-letter word that had given me sleepless nights—LOVE (what did you think?).

It was time to move from the four-letter "L" word to the four-letter "F" word. Definitely wouldn't mind those sleepless nights.

One day, a colleague named Mohit invited me to a Halloween party. I was in two minds because I'm not much of a costume party kind of guy. Then again, it was the only invite I had for that weekend. So after some deliberation, I decided to go.

Although I was very apprehensive, I ordered a skeleton costume to look the part. I even painted my face white, with black patches around my eyes, nose, and mouth. I was impressed with myself for the effort I'd put into a fancy dress party I wouldn't have even considered attending a year ago.

I arrived at Mohit's house at 9:00 PM, and most of the guests were already there. The problem (or perhaps the blessing) with such cosplay parties is that you can't even recognize the people you know.

I was amazed to see that people had gone the extra mile to dress up for this gathering. From daggers popping out of their hearts to bat wings sprouting out of dresses, I found myself almost judging them for having nothing better to do.

As I moved around the room, I was greeted by a yeti, twin witches, and an ogre whose spandex costume appeared to be at least two sizes too small (wasn't prepared to see those bulges).

"I didn't know these cosplay parties were such a rage," I thought to myself.

Since I could hardly recognize anyone and Mohit's phone wasn't reachable either, I decided to head to the bar area. And by the bar, I mean a table on which a large coffin-like tub was placed, filled with what looked like blood.

I took a cup and drank a sip, only to realize it was a fruit punch infused with vodka. "Well, something to keep me company this evening," I thought.

My eyes scanned the room, hoping to find a familiar face. But alas! There was none (I blame the dingy setup and the painted faces). I realized that such parties weren't really meant for me. I couldn't even expect to meet someone here. Who knows what she'd look like when the clothes came off? I mean, the clothes *and* makeup.

Suddenly, the DJ amped up the music, and a group of girls shrieked as they ran towards the dance floor. The real anti-social me was taking over, and I realized I couldn't bear all the noise. I placed my half-full cup on a nearby table and decided to dash for the door.

Just then, I laid eyes on someone.

She was wearing a tight black corset paired with a short red skirt and a bunny-ears headband. While I couldn't figure out which Halloween character she was dressed as I definitely knew it wasn't from a child-friendly novel.

She and two of her girlfriends were dancing unabashedly, and although I was initially drawn to her, it didn't take me long to start judging her based on her wild demeanour.

I still had remnants of the old, conservative me deep down. Why was she dressed so boldly?

But she was undeniably attractive. There was something unconventionally appealing about this girl. Why *was* I fascinated by her? Even the music suddenly seemed to fade out, and the world around me began to move in slow-motion (so filmi!).

But I'm not the type to make a pass at strange women. So, I started heading towards the main door when my friend Mohit appeared out of nowhere.

"Where were you, Abhay? I thought you weren't coming. Come, let me introduce you to a few people."

Mohit noticed that I wasn't making eye contact with him and was constantly looking in that girl's direction.

"Abhay, who are you ogling at?"

"Who? Me? No! Let's go."

"No, no. Let's get this over with. Let me introduce you to Kaavya."

"KAAVYA," shouted Mohit as he vigorously waved in the girls' direction. Kaavya looked at Mohit, and as he beckoned her, she started walking towards us with her friends.

"Kaavya, this is Abhay, and he was totally checking you out. But then again, can you blame him?" Mohit said, giving her a lecherous look.

I was shocked that someone was actually saying these words.

Thankfully, Kaavya wasn't taken aback. "Stop being a creep, Mohit."

"Hi, I'm Kaavya. Nice to meet you."

"Hello, I'm Abhay," I said nervously, shaking her hand and introducing myself.

"So, what do you do, Abhay?"

"I'm a digital marketing manager, and I work at an ad agency," I replied, feeling a bit weak-kneed.

"Great. I'm a photographer with the Animal Empire channel."

She had such a captivating gaze that I just couldn't look away.

"So do you want to touch it?"

I couldn't believe my ears.

"Umm…touch what?"

"My amulet that you've been staring at."

She took my hand and placed it on her chest. "This is an Egyptian amulet. Doesn't it look great with my ensemble?"

"Yeah, it's nice."

I gulped. Definitely wasn't used to such candour.

"Come, let's have shots," she said, taking my hand and leading me to the bar area.

Before I knew it, I was back in this dimly lit corner they called a 'bar'. What were the chances?

But I was *even* more surprised by Kaavya's shots-consumption capacity. It was definitely twice as much as mine, if not more.

"Do you want to hang out sometime? I'm having a card party at my house next week."

I could tell she was a little intoxicated by now. Her voice was slurred, and as she leaned closer to me, I could smell the alcohol from a distance.

Quite frankly, I was taken aback by her in-my-face boldness.

I nodded politely and excused myself, pretending to attend a call.

Something was different. I was overcome with a sudden rush of emotions.

Was it just the ambience or something in my drink?

Just then, Mohit came running towards me, putting his hirsute arm (no, that wasn't part of his costume) around my neck.

"Oh boy! Aren't you a lucky man?"

"What do you mean, bro?" I asked.

"Well, don't you know? That's Kaavya. She was the most popular girl in my college. I've had *the* biggest crush on her since then, but she doesn't pay me any heed."

"Good for you man. She doesn't seem to be my type."

"Not your type? Smart, sexy, feisty…isn't your type?"

"Not really, man. You should go for her. I'll be heading out."

While I didn't care much for Mohit's recommendation, why *was* I attracted to this girl?

It must be a side effect of my endless dry spell. I'm sure there wasn't more to it.

As I hurried towards the main door, my head and heart were screaming, "Definitely not her!"

CHAPTER 3
MAYBE HER

It was the first week of November. I distinctly remember because there was a nip in the air, and I had to stay back and work on an important, time-sensitive presentation. It was 6:30 PM, but it was already pitch dark outside. I picked up my laptop and decided to sit in the office café for the rest of the evening.

Suddenly, my phone rang, and I saw an unknown number flashing on the phone screen. I answered the call, and before I could say anything, the caller said, “Hey Abhay. Guess who?”

Although I recognized it was a girl's voice, I couldn't place it. “I’m sorry, I don’t have your number saved. Who’s this?”

“This is Kaavya! We met at Mohit's Halloween party. Don’t you remember?”

I had been going about my life as usual and had completely forgotten about my encounter with Kaavya the other night.

Okay, I'm lying. I did think about her a few times since then. But I couldn't fathom why.

"Oh yes, how are you?"

"All well. Let's skip the formality and cut to the chase."

Not quite following what she meant, I just nodded inquisitively. Although later I realized that she wouldn't have seen my frantic neck movement through the phone.

"I have a card party at my place next Saturday, and you should come."

"But, I might have…another plan," I replied instantly.

I knew I had no prior engagement, but there was this funny feeling in my stomach that made me a bit uncomfortable (okay, it could've also been the burrito I had for lunch).

Also, let's not forget that despite my recent spree of party-hopping, I needed some time to decide if I wanted to go to a party where I'd met the host once for all of 10 minutes.

"I'm not taking no for an answer. I'll text you my address. See you at 8."

"Okay. I'll surely try."

"No, you *have* to come. Oh, and yes, there's a dress code too."

"What's the dress code? Ethnic wear?"

"No, I'm not that cliché. Just come as your sexiest best. Shouldn't be too hard for you," she giggled.

I turned red!

I'm just glad this was a phone conversation, and no one could see me blushing.

Although this new girl from HR sitting a few tables away did seem to be amused, looking at my shifty behaviour.

"Just kidding. Got to go, Abhay. See you on Saturday. Bye!"

I was sceptical about attending Kaavya's party, especially since I barely knew her and it was at her house. But as you know, I had been on a socializing spree lately, so I decided to go for a bit. What's the worst that could happen?

In my heart of hearts, I wanted to look impressive too (given the not-so-subtle dress code). So I wore my new blue denim and paired it with a black suede jacket. I don't know what prompted me, but I reached for my finest cologne, and I sprayed it on.

I looked into the mirror, and mamma mia, I was quite happy with what I saw.

To avoid arriving too early, I waited for a while, receiving occasional stares from my mom, and reached Kaavya's house at 8:45 PM.

I rang the doorbell and patiently waited. Minutes later, the door opened, and there stood Kaavya, dressed in what seemed to be a night suit.

"Abhay, what are *you* doing here?"

"I came to your party. Is it already over?"

Kaavya burst out laughing. “It’s not today, silly. It’s next Saturday.”

“Damn, that’s embarrassing. I should have read your message more carefully.”

“That’s fine. Now that you’re here, why don’t you come inside.”

Since I’d already spent over an hour driving to her house, I thought I might as well spend some time before heading back home. So I gladly obliged and stepped inside.

Her house was huge! It somehow didn’t seem that big from the outside, but once I entered, it felt like I was standing in the lobby of a five-star hotel.

As I walked in, I saw an ornate, golden chandelier laden with crystals, hanging from the ceiling. Below it was the living room, adorned with dove-colored sofas and a massive beige teakwood table.

I was visibly impressed but tried to conceal my true feelings.

For a few moments, I was lost in the sheer beauty of this architectural marvel right in front of me.

Suddenly, I heard Kaavya's voice, “I’ll give you a tour of the house later. Let’s sit in my room.”

She lightly held my hand, and we started walking towards the staircase. I felt a current running through my body.

“Must be my overactive hormones,” I thought.

After climbing what seemed like the staircase to heaven, we reached her room.

Her room was very different from the rest of her house. While the house had more muted shades of white and beige, her room had splashes of colour everywhere.

Lush green planters, bright pink dream catchers, and picturesque paintings of animals and birds adorned the space.

“I painted these myself,” she said.

“They’re beautiful.”

She pointed to a photo wall displaying a collage of pictures from all around the world.

“I took that one in Africa. This one’s from Egypt. Oh, and that’s my favourite one from my impromptu trip to Jordan.”

“Impromptu?” I asked, looking at the pictures with admiration.

“Yeah, one day I randomly decided to go to Jordan. No one agreed to come along, so I just went by myself. I was on a flight within 3 hours of taking that call.”

She giggled, “I can be a bit impulsive sometimes.”

Kaavya showed me around, and it was evident that she was extremely passionate about nature and wildlife.

“You seem to have travelled a lot already.”

“Yes, I *love* to travel. I’m crazy about nature and photography.”

She continued, “The reason why I’m working at the Animal Empire channel is that I get to travel the world and be up close and personal with wildlife.”

"Amazing. That's why you seem to be really wild…I mean passionate about the wild."

"Haha! That's alright. I don't mind that. I am quite the wildling."

"Speaking of wild," Kaavya continued, "there's no one at home today."

I turned red yet again.

"Want to do something fun?"

Why did every other thing she say make me blush?

I mustered up the courage and asked, "What do you have in mind?"

"It'll involve some jumps, bumps, and a whole lot of sweating."

She had a mysterious grin on her face, and I could already feel beads of sweat forming on my forehead (it was 10 degrees outside).

"Sure," I said faintly.

We went downstairs into a quaint, dark room. Hormones were blazing through my body.

"Tada! Welcome to my virtual reality arena."

For the uninitiated, VR is this incredible technology that can create a make-believe world where you can do interesting things: right from virtually travelling the world and playing games to attending conferences and concerts.

No, I'm not a part-time VR salesperson. It's a part of my day job as a digital marketer, remember?

But what did she have in mind for the both of us today?

"We're going to have a dance-off. Here you go."

She handed me a virtual reality headset and I started to put it on with trembling hands.

"I'm not much of a dancer," I said.

"That's alright. Just keep your body loose and let the music take over."

"THREE. TWO. ONE. ROUND ONE BEGINS."

Her music system had surround sound, and soon the room was filled with loud music.

I was supposed to follow the movements prompted by the game, but I was too conscious.

Kaavya was obviously winning.

I tried to keep up, but it was very difficult. Not only did I have two left feet, but I also couldn't concentrate.

"I'm so going to destroy you, Abhay!" said Kaavya in a shrill voice. "That's the beauty of dance. Stop overthinking and just go with the flow."

She did make sense and soon enough I was grooving to the music. Even though my steps didn't match the choreography, I was having a great time.

The score was 3-0 and it was time for the last and final round.

"ROUND 4: COUPLE DANCE."

As you may have realized by now, I'm usually slow on the uptake. I was puzzled as always and was dancing on the spot when I suddenly felt a hand on my chest.

"We have to do this together, silly."

I was pretty sweaty, and I didn't want to get too close but Kaayva already had one hand placed firmly on my shoulder and the other just above my waist.

I, too, put my arm around her, and we danced to an old English ballad for a straight 2 minutes. This was probably the most in sync I'd ever been in my life.

I didn't want this moment to end.

What was so charismatic about her? Why was she drawing me to herself like a moth to a flame?

Her fun, authentic self was a refreshing change from the people I'd been with all my life. Could that be it?

Since my vision was obstructed by the headset, I probably had more confidence in pulling this off than if I had been looking straight into her eyes.

The song ended and Kaavya was in my arms, leaning backward.

I removed my headset, and so did she. Our noses were almost touching. We were both panting and out of breath.

She closed her eyes, and I don't know what got into me, but I leaned forward and gave her a light kiss.

It's very unusual for me to do such a thing but it just felt right. *She* didn't move back either.

After a few seconds, I opened my eyes and pulled away.

Kaavya had a smile on her face as she opened her eyes. For the first time, I saw her blush.

Had we swapped personalities?

I returned the smile and awkwardly looked away.

"I think I should get going now," I said, walking hurriedly towards the staircase that led upstairs.

"Yes, sure," she spoke in such a calm, serene voice. It didn't sound like her for a minute.

We were both quiet as we walked towards the entrance of her house.

She'd never been so quiet before. I assumed she might be a little embarrassed too, so I didn't say anything. Not that I could either because my mind was already corrupted with all kinds of thoughts.

Who was this girl? Where did she come from all of a sudden? She was bringing out an interesting colour in my personality that I didn't even know existed.

"Alright then. Thanks for the evening, Kaavya."

"You're welcome. See you."

I really wanted to say more, maybe even stay for a bit longer. But I didn't know how to react after the recent developments.

I turned and started walking towards the porch where my car was parked.

Just then Kaavya broke the silence. "Abhay!" I turned back.

"You know my parents are travelling for the entire week."

She smirked. I smirked.

The Kaavya I knew was back. But what was wrong with me?

She was unlike any girl on my checklist, but I still wanted to go back to her.

Why *was* I drawn to her? Was she like the forbidden fruit that was out of bounds? Was it just infatuation? Or was I really falling for her?

Ah! This mysterious girl, her adorable antics, and our first kiss. I couldn't think about anything else on my way back home.

CHAPTER 4
DEFINITELY HER!

I did not go to Kaavya's house that week.

Alright, I went once.

Fine, twice.

Okay, all the three times I went, it was amazing!

Kaavya and I were *very* different people. I'd like to think of myself as a calm, practical guy who likes to plan things out and be more organized in life.

Kaavya, on the other hand, was the complete opposite. She was bright, vibrant, and a true believer in living life to the fullest. She didn't have inhibitions and would just go with the flow rather than overthink things.

Maybe I was attracted to her only because she was so different from me.

Whatever the reason, every time I was with her, I would literally have a blast. No pun intended there.

And I might be getting ahead of myself here, but she seemed *very* interested in me too.

Despite our apparent differences, we would spend hours together. From going out on dinner dates and chatting into the night to making out at her house and everywhere else, I was having the time of my life.

She told me stories about her childhood and how she grew up with strict and proper parents (in other words, quite unlike her) who always wanted her to follow a certain preordained path.

"Dad always wanted me to grow up and join his business, but I never wanted to."

"And what about your mom?" I asked.

"Well, she didn't have much of a say either. It was always Dad's final word."

"Kaavya, do this, Kaavya, don't do that," she said mimicking her dad's voice. "For the first 15 years of my life, all my decisions were made *for* me. I just needed to break free from the rules."

For the first time since we started going out, I saw Kaavya's vulnerable side.

I could understand what made her the so-called rebel who wanted to do the exact opposite of what was prescribed to her by her parents. But deep down, I believed Kaavya was still a dutiful girl, petrified by her parents. She just covered it up really well.

The best quality about Kaavya was that she didn't think ahead and complicate things. She knew how to live in the moment, and this time around, I too was planning to do just that.

We were taking this one step at a time and quite frankly we both knew this was a short-term relationship.

I guess that's why I was loving it so much.

Kaavya was like a breath of fresh air and because of her, I'd totally forgotten about my past woes.

Best of all, I knew Kaavya was not a typical girl who wanted to get married or have kids, so I thought life was just perfect!

Or was it?

It had been a few weeks since we started going out, and for our next date, I chose a beautiful rooftop café overlooking a quaint lake—the perfect spot for a winter afternoon tête-à-tête.

We both ordered hot chocolate, and I was giving ideas about where we could sneak off the following weekend.

"Where is this relationship heading, Abhay?"

"Umm…Kaavya?"

"I know we don't really talk about this ever. But I still need to know. For *my* sake."

"Well, I really like spending time with you. You know that. But I haven't thought about our future yet."

"I get that but do you even want a future?"

"I'm not sure. I mean, I thought you didn't either. Why are we suddenly talking about this?"

"You know how my parents are right. They've been pestering me to get married and last night I just happened to mention you to them."

The last I knew, Kaavya was defying everything her parents said so why this sudden turn of events?

"What exactly did you tell them?"

"Nothing. I just said I'm seeing someone and I'm definitely not meeting boys right now because I might already be with the one."

I nearly choked on my hot chocolate.

"Don't worry. Of course, I don't mean that. You don't have to be under any pressure to make a decision."

"But," she continued, "we can't just keep seeing each other without knowing if there's any future for us."

I was perplexed because I didn't see Kaayva as someone who would want to be in a long-term, committed relationship.

"See Abhay, you don't have to decide right now. But take some time and let me know if we're just fooling around or if there's more to this."

I could see her tearing up, and I just wasn't ready for this emotional outburst.

I was right! As I anticipated, deep down, Kaavya was her parents' goody-two-shoes daughter who was probably done playing the rebel.

Kaavya stood up, smiled, and walked away. I was left sitting there alone, wondering.

I did *not* see this coming.

I knew I had to get back to her, though. We were at an awkward crossroads in our relationship, and I owed her an answer.

Did I love spending time with her? Most definitely, yes. And we were having a lot of fun too.

But I had to decide if this relationship was like a one-night stand or a marriage, quite literally.

Why did Kaavya have to bring in this unnecessary complexity when everything was going well? I couldn't sleep that night, so I decided to really break it down for myself.

Was I having a great time because Kaavya was a fun, uninhibited person and so unlike me? Perhaps!

Was I just assuming this was a short-term relationship and hence liked not having to commit? That does sound like me.

Was it because of the great sex? No, that couldn't be it. Well, maybe a little bit.

Was it because of her huge house? Oh, dear Lord, I hope not. Alright, 10% because of that too.

But the real question was: Could I picture myself being with her for the *rest* of my life? Or was it okay for me to walk away while there was still time?

My mind was overflowing with thoughts about everything that I'd grown up believing, everything I'd been taught, and everything I'd expected from my life partner.

I was overwhelmed by the barrage of questions popping into my head.

Isn't she so different from me? So wild and adventurous.

She hardly ticks any of the boxes from my checklist (remember I had a checklist?).

What would my parents say? They would probably never approve of her.

What about my friends and family? They'd think I've married her only for her money.

Will she settle well in my house? Her career is surely going to keep her busy.

It was at this precise moment I decided to kill all this chatter in my mind and listen to someone who never lies to me.

Someone who has my best interest at heart and would never misguide me—ME!

Shhh! Tuning into Ab-hay 2.0 FM.

In today's episode, Abhay will reveal how he *truly* feels about Kaavya…

Undoubtedly, the last few weeks with Kaavya had been nothing short of magical.

I was avoiding the impending question because of the fun and games, but let's face it even I needed to know where we were headed.

I felt like she completed me, and I completed her. Since the first time we met, it just seemed right. It's hard to put this feeling in words but something clicked.

Was this love? That can't be it. It was too soon to be love.

Or was it? Who's to say that love can only happen after a certain amount of time?

As soon as that awareness came to me, the answer was glaring in my face.

I can't believe it took me this long to realize, but the decision was clear.

I couldn't believe I'd found the person who I could spend hours listening to without getting bored. The person who'd make me feel good about myself. The person who I wanted to take care of, protect and love with all that I have, forever and ever.

Wow, I'm sounding like a hopeless romantic. But that's what love does to you, doesn't it?

It felt like my head and my heart said to me in unison that she indeed was THE ONE.

CHAPTER 5
REALLY HER?

"My parents would like to host you for dinner this Sunday."

I was shocked out of my wits.

I'd barely come to terms with the fact that I was going ahead with the proposition of committing to someone. I didn't imagine I'd already be asked to meet with the parents.

Don't blame me. It hadn't even been 24 hours since I called Kaavya and told her about my feelings.

Quick recap: I'd been evidently disturbed after my last conversation with Kaavya and after some serious introspection, I knew how I truly felt. All I needed to do now was tell her about my feelings.

However, during this period of turbulence, I didn't do a great job of concealing my true emotions from my parents. They too had noticed something was wrong.

So I told them about Kaavya and the fact that I was *pretty* certain that she was the one for me.

Both my parents were overjoyed. My mom almost burst into tears, partly because she was happy and partly because she knew how long it had taken her sonny boy to finally find his soulmate.

"When are we meeting her? Let's meet this weekend. Should I order your favourite 'kaju barfi' to send to the neighbours?"

"Mom, Dad! Will you please relax? We're taking things slow. I'll let you know when the time comes."

"Oh slow it seems? How old are you, again? Do I need to remind you that all your friends and cousins are already married," said my mom sarcastically.

"I knew I shouldn't have told you anything."

My father was surprisingly calm. "It's fine, *beta*. We're excited to meet her whenever you'd like."

As dramatic as this episode was, having my parents' consent further solidified my decision, and in that excitement I video-called Kaavya.

"Hi, love! How've you been?"

"I'm fine, Abhay. Was waiting for your call."

"I know it's late but I just had to tell you this. Here goes! I really *really* love you."

I continued, "You make me the happiest man in the world and you're the only person I'd want to be with."

Kaavya sighed. "I love you too, Abhay. I never thought I'd meet someone like you," she said with a trembling voice.

We looked at each other through our handheld devices and hoped to capture this moment in time.

I literally took a screenshot of this moment on my phone for memory's sake.

She almost cried. I definitely did.

We met the next day and we weren't just a no-strings-attached couple anymore. Strings were very much attached now.

We sat and spoke about the amazing moments we'd created in the past few weeks, and how excited we were to create more memorable experiences together in the times to come.

However, just before Kaavya stepped out of my car that evening, she happened to mention how her parents wanted to meet me.

"My parents would like to host you for dinner this Sunday."

I was perplexed!

I'd somehow managed to convince my parents that while we were in love, we didn't want to rush into anything.

And there I was in another dilemma about meeting Kaavya's parents.

This was moving all too fast.

"But Kaavya, what's the rush? I thought you'll be happy that we're planning to spend our lives together. Why do I have to meet your parents *already*?"

"Don't worry. It's going to be a casual meeting. They just want to know you better. That's all."

"I'm not sure about this."

"I'll be honest, baby. You know the equation I've had with my parents. While trying to carve out my own path, I kept disregarding their feelings. I owe this to them."

"Don't go all emo on me now. I too want a future with you but why do I have to meet them now?"

"Trust me. What can possibly happen? They're not going to force you to marry me."

"So when are you both planning to get married?" asked Kaavya's dad, Mr. Singhania.

Kaavya's dad, Mr. Harvansh Singhania, was a tall, broad man who had a loud, larger-than-life personality.

Kaavya's mom Mrs. Kavita Singhania, on the other hand, was a petite, elegant woman.

It was clear where Kaavya got her good looks from.

Mrs. Singhania interrupted her husband, "He's just got here. Let's not make him uncomfortable."

I breathed a sigh of relief.

"I think you both should get engaged now. You can marry anytime during the auspicious wedding season in winter," she continued.

My heart started to race again.

Why do I land myself in such peculiar situations?

I looked at Kaavya. She wasn't making eye contact for obvious reasons.

I knew she was petrified by her parents. She felt she had defied them all her life. And it was only recently that they'd come to terms with her decisions and even started complimenting her on her passion for photography.

So I couldn't expect her to contradict them now and stand up for me.

Maybe she secretly wanted to get married too. Why else would she play along and not voice her opinion even once?

I was furious, in equal parts, at Kaavya and at myself.

At Kaavya for keeping me in the dark, knowing exactly what her parents had in mind for this meeting. And at myself for agreeing to willingly walk into this trap.

I started to wonder if I'd made a mistake by re-initiating the chapter of marriage in my life.

I was happy and complete even before I met Kaavya, wasn't I?

There was a (not so happy) sinking feeling inside me that I couldn't comprehend.

Was I just afraid to commit? Or had I been hurt way too many times in the past to be scared to fall in love and make a commitment?

I couldn't understand whether it was me trying to run away from the situation because of my experiences or whether I was scared to finally be in a perfectly happy relationship.

In the midst of all the chaos in my head, I did know one thing for sure - Kaavya could have handled the situation better.

“You should definitely get hitched before she gets her next project in some corner of the world,” said Kaavya’s mom.

Kaavya’s dad intervened, “Oh and we’ll be sponsoring the honeymoon. Any place of your choice in business class son.”

Should I tell them that the ‘honey’ from the honeymoon had been spilled? Several times over.

Perhaps not. I just nodded politely.

Thankfully, there was no conclusion in terms of dates for the wedding or the engagement.

I used my parents as an excuse to buy more time and dodge all questions that came my way.

“Uncle, I’ve been very close with my parents. I don’t think I can decide anything without their consent and blessing.” I almost conjured a fake tear as I said this.

“Oh, absolutely son! We should meet again with your parents soon.”

I would have agreed to anything at that point as long as I could escape from that torture cell.

I knew exactly how “soon” I wanted the next meeting to happen.

The awkward meeting with her parents finally came to an end. I could see Kaavya trying to say something to me from the corner of my eye.

But I ignored her pursuit and continued to walk steadily towards the door.

More often than not I've found myself sprinting out of her house at full speed. I'm not sure what that says about our relationship.

Anyway, whatever my dilemma, I realized one thing as I stepped out of her house - I'd probably said yes too soon.

CHAPTER 6
SAID YES TOO SOON

"I'm sorry, Abhay. I've apologized to you like a thousand times. What more do you want me to say?"

I'd been dodging Kaavya's calls and messages, and we were finally talking on the phone after three days. But I still chose to answer in single syllables.

Don't judge me. I'm only human!

I was obviously livid. At Kaavya's home, I was caught off guard without the slightest clue of how serious this meeting would turn out to be.

And Kaavya not only did not forewarn me, she almost played along with them.

There I was sitting right underneath their elaborate chandelier, hoping against hope that it would just fall on me and end this drama.

I needed her to know I wasn't okay with this. And being the private person that I am, I needed time to process what had just transpired.

At some level, I also wanted her to go through the same anguish that I'd gone through. That's why I needed to cut her off for a while.

"You've been avoiding my calls. You aren't replying to my texts. I'm sorry, I really didn't know my parents would react like this."

"Yeah, right," I retorted.

"Fine! If you don't want to believe me there's nothing more I can do. At least say something so I know you care about this."

"There's nothing to say."

"I can't believe you, Abhay. I said I'm sorry. This can't be the end for us."

At this point, my heart had just about started to melt. And let's be honest, I was missing her too.

But I wouldn't have had a problem with her feeling bad for a *bit* longer. While it had been three days and she'd really tried to patch things up, I wasn't done yet.

"Do you even realize how humiliating this was for me? Not once did you take my side, Kaavya. And you've not even met my parents."

"Oh, we'll meet them. Of course, their approval matters too."

I interjected, "It didn't seem so. Aren't they as important as yours? You think your rich father can just *buy* me with his business class ticket and fancy vintage car?"

Oops, that was a tad below the belt. I needed to do some damage control quickly.

Before I could say anything, Kaavya took a deep breath and said, "What did you just say, Abhay? I think that's your insecurity talking."

"My insecurity? At least I don't have to pretend to be someone else in front of my parents. I'm not fake like you!"

"Now you've really crossed the line! I can't believe I thought I had a future with you. I definitely don't want to be with someone who has no respect for me and my family. I'm done with you, Abhay."

Suddenly I didn't even have a few syllables left in my dictionary.

"Wait, what?"

"Of course! If you're not ready to be in an adult relationship, then don't be in one. I am not desperate to get married either, least of all to *you*!"

I felt the world around me swirling. What had just happened? I felt a horrible flutter in my stomach.

Okay fine, I felt really uncomfortable being in the situation Kaavya's parents had put me in. And yes, as much as I hate to admit it, I was loving all the attention I was getting from her after that incident.

But I definitely didn't think we would break up because of that!

Hadn't I already started talking about upgrading our relationship status?

Here I was thinking this wasn't even my fault and everyone should make *me* feel nice. And suddenly, the next moment, I was clueless about how this had spiralled out of control and left me single, yet again.

I know I said things I shouldn't have. But she knows that's how I react when I'm fuming. I obviously didn't mean any of that; a lot of it was just for effect. She did know that, right?

Oh, man! Was I really not meant to be in a relationship? Was I just wanting a long-term commitment because I was conditioned to be in one since I was younger?

I don't think that's true though. My feelings for Kaavya transcended that. I was *so* confused.

But what about our fallout? She made it clear she didn't want this relationship anymore. Was there any going back or was the damage too grave?

Someone tell me what to do next. If only there were a cheat sheet!

CHAPTER 7
I DO! DO I?

While I didn't have a well-thought-out plan in place, one thing was clear - I wasn't ready to lose Kaavya at any cost.

There was this strong feeling inside that was killing me for not fixing this in time. But where do I even start?

Probably by telling her that I didn't think of this as a casual relationship.

I guess I just didn't realize how much I loved her!

My God, really? Even after this massive fight?

Yes! I did.

This *must* be true love. Much like how you see in movies; despite all obstacles, against all odds.

Except, I was the obstacle in my own story.

What was I doing? I needed to tell her. The very thought of not being with her, not holding her, not speaking to her, was driving me crazy.

I clearly never felt this way about *anyone* before.

"Alright then, Abhay. It's time to grow up and take matters into your own hands," I said to myself while looking into the mirror.

What would be a good way to let her know I cared about her and that her happiness meant the world to me?

I needed to conjure a reason that was strong enough for her to speak to me again.

I almost thought of faking an injury, but I realized that would make her even more mad once she'd learnt the truth.

I thought and thought, and it finally dawned on me. I knew what I had to do.

I made all the preparations I needed to make.

Was I nervous? Hell, yes! But I just had to make the gesture grand and memorable. Sometimes I still can't believe *I* pulled that off.

I told Kaavya I wanted to meet with her just once. But I didn't tell her why.

Instead, I made up a reason that I knew she couldn't say no to.

At first, she didn't answer my calls (karma, I guess). But after a few (read many) incessant attempts, I succeeded.

I told her my office was looking for a high-end photographer and since their photographer had ditched them at the last minute (so fake), they were desperate to get someone on short notice.

If there was anything Kaavya loved more than anything in the world, it was her work.

She wasn't keen on the gig at first for obvious reasons.

But I knew she had a good heart and so after a bit of resistance, she agreed.

I told her to carry a few dressy clothes too for the soirée later that evening, after which I promised to drop her home.

To make the set-up look believable I took a "junior" photographer with me in the car to help her out through the day.

I told her the shoot location was a little far so I'd pick her up at six in the morning. I reached five minutes early and waited patiently in the car with my accomplice.

I saw Kaavya walk down her porch. Even in something as simple as a pale pink jumpsuit, she looked stunning.

I could almost see cupids flying from either side but I needed to keep a straight face.

"Hi Abhay, how have you been?" she asked softly.

"I've been okay. This is Kumar. He's going to be helping you with the shoot today."

"You told me the shoot is for a wildlife-inspired clothing line. But I'd need to know more than that."

"Don't worry," I said. "You'll get the entire brief once we get there."

Kaavya nodded. But she didn't talk much on the way. I knew she was still bummed.

I, on the other hand, was both excited and nervous to carry out my plan.

For the first time in my life, taking this giant leap felt right!

The venue was three hours away and we reached well in time.

As soon as we were getting out of the car I looked at Kumar and gave him a nudge. He knew exactly what to do.

I told Kaavya if she could stay back for a few minutes and much to my surprise, she obliged.

"I know we're here for work and to not discuss personal matters. But all I want to say is that I'm very sorry."

"But Abhay," Kaavya intervened.

"Please Kaavya, just give me thirty more seconds. It's not easy for me to do this either. But I can't imagine my life without you and whatever you decide to do after this, I just want you to know that I'm not afraid anymore. You are the only person who makes me believe in love and I don't want to lose you come what may. That's all."

Kaavya smiled. I could see a glint in her eye.

I know she wanted to hear this and was beaming from inside as I expressed my true feelings.

What was even more shocking was that I didn't feel scared even for a second while blurting out my well-rehearsed monologue.

Kaavya looked at me with a comforting glance. I knew I was making progress.

I smiled back at her and we started to walk inside. It was time for my glorious plan to come into play.

And quite frankly, the plan would have fallen flat on its face had Kaavya not warmed up to me after my little speech.

The venue was a beautiful, old palace that had been converted into a luxurious resort.

As we started to walk up the stairs, we could hear a flautist playing a beautiful melody.

Moments later, he was joined by other artists and the soulful sound of the flute, sitar, and tabla filled the corridors.

Of course, Kaavya had no idea all of this was for her.

As we climbed onto the last stair, Kaavya was greeted by a group of artists standing on either side of the pathway that led to the palace gate.

One of them was a singer who started crooning tunes from Indian classical ragas.

I already felt goosebumps all over my body. But I almost forgot this entire spectacle was not for me so I turned towards Kaavya.

I could observe her reaction as she seemed both confused and excited.

Kumar was at a distance capturing all of these golden moments for us (yes, he came along for a reason).

As we continued to walk, we could feel a shower of fresh petals on us.

I knew they were lilies because I'd paid for them (through my nose, if I may add). Soon enough, we were walking on a bed of lilies.

Oh, it was just so romantic!

I was hoping Kaavya felt the same way too. I knew she loved Indian classical music and grand historic sites, so the chances of this not going right were slim.

But it surpassed even my expectations. I was more than satisfied with how it turned out.

"I'm loving the entire vibe of this place," I said loudly as Kaavya nodded in agreement.

It indeed *was* a perfect winter morning and the atmosphere that had been created was nothing short of magical.

Finally, as we entered the Great Hall we saw a burst of colour through the room - vibrant hues of red, green, and yellow. This dramatic effect was courtesy of the coloured smoke bombs that were lined on either side of the entrance.

It was a picture-perfect moment - straight out of a colourful Hindi movie!

But that's not all folks.

It was time for the grand reveal - huge drapes of satin unfurled before us and on them was written: *Kaavya, I love you!*

I looked at Kaavya. She was beaming with excitement.

My vision was a little blurry because I was welling up. Kaavya, on the other hand, was just smiling ear to ear and gave me a tight hug.

I knew all the effort had been worth it.

I just hoped Kumar, our dear photographer, captured all these precious moments perfectly.

"So *this* was your grand plan? You cheeky little boy," said Kaavya.

"I love you, Kaavya. And I really am sorry. I won't let you go away *ever*."

"Aww!" She gave me a quick peck and immediately looked around the room to see who all saw us.

Seeing Kaavya being her happy, goofy self gave me a great sense of relief.

I thanked all the staff and artists who'd helped me organize this surprise and we went upstairs to check into our room.

In case you were wondering: yes, Kumar was in another room and no, there was no real brand shoot planned.

I knew I would get some good loving that day. And boy, I sure did.

After spending the next few hours canoodling each other, I knew I had to execute the GRAND FINALE.

Yes, this was just the first act. The finale was underway.

While Kaavya was still in bed, I snuck out to check if everything was in order.

When I came back to the room half an hour later she was up but still in bed. I could see the glow on her face.

"Where were you?"

"I'd just gone to check on Kumar. All's well."

Her sun-kissed hair fell lightly over her face as she got up and walked towards me wearing my shirt, with a cup in her hand.

"Ah! I could get used to this view," I thought.

"Coffee? With 2 spoons of sugar, just the way you like it," she said lovingly.

"Thanks, babe."

She handed me the cup, sat on my thigh, and just watched me sip my coffee. I too was deliberately drinking slowly because I didn't want this moment to end.

But I knew there was something even more special in store. It was time for *the* final act.

CHAPTER 8
SHE SAID YES!

I told Kaavya to get dressed so we could go for a walk around the beautiful property.

I also convinced her that we should get a few professional pictures clicked since the ones in the morning were candid.

Being a photographer herself, she was very particular about getting the best photos and I took advantage of that.

She got dressed in a long, flowing yellow dress.

I was enamoured with her even more so if that was possible.

"Aren't you going to be cold?"

Of all the things in the world I could have said, I can't believe I said that.

"I'll be fine," she said as she pulled her hair behind her ears to wear earrings.

"Those are the ones I gifted!" I said, pleasantly surprised.

“Yes. Everything you’ve ever gifted is very special to me.”

I was turning red. It was like I was falling in love all over again.

What a feeling!

I too wore my finest tuxedo and frankly wasn’t looking half as bad myself.

“Shall we?” I asked by extending my hand. She held on to it firmly as we headed to the gardens.

I’d informed Kumar as well about our excursion so he’d do the needful and take our customary pictures while giving us the privacy we needed.

We reached the end of the garden where a long, narrow boat - which looked like a Gondola - waited for our arrival.

The gondolier was excited to see us and ushered us into the boat.

Kaavya was ecstatic and I too couldn’t have been happier myself. The boat ride was nothing short of enchanting and minutes later we reached our final destination.

As we walked through a narrow cobbled street, we came across a gazebo with a small wrought iron dining table under it.

The chef and the waiter were standing at a distance and greeted us with pleasant smiles.

I pulled out Kaavya’s chair and helped her get seated. I felt like such a gentleman. My ensemble really helped me amplify this feeling.

“This is such a pleasant surprise. Thank you!” Kaavya exclaimed.

“You’re most welcome, my love. I’m so glad we could create this experience together.”

I continued, “I hope you’re not mad at me anymore.”

“Of course not, Abhay. I don’t know if I’ve said this enough times but I too love you.”

She was right. She hadn’t said this enough.

But I didn’t want to infuriate her by agreeing to that, so I just nodded slowly.

Voila! It was time for our three-course meal.

For starters, we had the chicken and truffle tartlets with edamame. This was followed by garlic butter scallops with a side of beetroot jus.

Finally, we gorged on a slice of our favourite dark chocolate and salted caramel cake.

How much we loved our meal was evident from how quickly we polished off the dishes.

“Isn’t this just picture-perfect?” I asked.

This was also my cue to Kumar to click us but he was too busy staring into space to acknowledge my code.

I placed my hand on top of Kaavya’s and we were just looking into each other’s eyes.

Too full of love (and food) to be doing anything else.

Then suddenly we could hear music at a distance. It sounded like French jazz (had almost forgotten about that).

Since jazz was Kaavya's favourite, I made sure even the music was to her liking.

Could she have asked for a better boyfriend? I think not.

The melodious sound started to grow as we saw a group of musicians walking towards us. They stood around us in a circle and soon enough we were grooving to the music.

I'd forgotten Kaavya's love for dancing, but it all came rushing back when I saw her shake a leg in full swing (pun intended).

I almost wanted to remind her that this wasn't a dance party, but I couldn't.

So for a couple of awkward moments, I just stood patiently waiting for the music to stop.

Then it suddenly dawned on me that I had a sure-shot way of getting her attention.

I went down on one knee, took out a ring from my left pocket, and said what any man in that position is expected to say.

"Kaavya, will you marry me?"

Just then, the musicians behind me held up a giant placard that read "Kaavya, please be mine forever!"

I was obviously shaking. What had I just done? I hadn't even told my parents!

Kaavya had tears in her eyes. I too was choked with emotions, but I had a whole speech prepared.

"YES! I WILL!" she shouted.

Wait, what? I had a lot more to say.

Oh well, maybe another time. I got up and hugged her tightly.

Coloured smoke bombs filled the air with vibrant, rainbow-like hues.

I guess they had a few left from the morning.

I knew I would have to pay through my nose for such an elaborate proposal, but Kaavya's expression at that moment made it all worth it.

At last, it was finally done.

I felt happy, relieved, and most of all accomplished.

For the first time in my life, I wasn't scared. This seemed right and I was feeling like the luckiest man alive.

After a memorable day, our third wheel Kumar, Kaavya and I came back to the city.

I dropped Kaavya home and gave her a parting kiss. I dropped Kumar home and did *not* give him a parting kiss.

I finally reached home dazed yet excited, only to start dreaming about my perfect love story.

I could barely sleep that night. All I did was thank my stars, for SHE SAID YES!

CHAPTER 9
I SAID NO!

"Bali would be just *perfect* in March!"

Kaavya continued, "Imagine our wedding nuptials being performed by the beach at sunset. It'll be magical."

"Umm, no Kaavya. Ain't happening!"

"I can't believe you don't want this dream wedding, Abhay. What's wrong with you?"

Me? What's wrong with *her*?

After the grand proposal, I thought we'd enjoy our courtship for a couple of weeks or even months.

But the die had been cast. There was no turning back now.

"Kaavya, you're meeting my parents the day after. Can we please focus on that?"

Remember I told you how I thought Kaavya was different from other girls I'd been with? And that our love story was unique and one for keeps.

Well, I was clearly mistaken.

Either that, or like a lot of women Kaavya too got overly emotional about her own wedding and wanted it to be as conventional as possible.

Whatever the case, I was screwed.

"Abhay, tell me something honestly. Will you marry me even if your parents say no?"

"Where is this coming from, Kaavya?"

"No, I just want to know for my sake."

Of course, I couldn't tell her that I wouldn't want to go against my parents' wishes, nor would I want to lose her. So I just had to hope it didn't come to that.

Although my parents probably didn't even have an option anymore now that Kaavya was wearing my family's heirloom ring (and honestly, neither did I).

I was just grateful that my mom hadn't noticed that the ring was missing.

The day for Kaavya to meet my parents finally came. And it was even more uneventful than I'd imagined it to be.

Kaavya came wearing a simple kurta and jeans. I didn't even tell her to but she wanted to impress my parents from the get-go.

Somewhere in the middle of the conversation, my mom tried to be funny, "Oh, with Kaavya here, we won't need a photographer for any of the functions now."

I thought that would irk Kaavya. But instead, she laughed at the 'joke' heartily.

They chatted for hours as though they'd known each other since the beginning of time.

"What a great start to the year," said my father. While I was glad to have brought this happiness upon them, I felt they were *too* happy for this alliance.

I mean, did they think I was so unlovable that I'd never get married?

I'm not saying I'm disappointed that the meeting went well, but I was deferring all wedding decisions to be taken post this rendezvous.

So at some level, I wanted at least a bit of drama to spice things up, but to no avail.

Anyway, with this obstacle also out of the way, all that was left to do was plan the wedding. Which, if I may add, is a herculean task in itself.

For starters, it's not always easy to be on the same page, especially with someone who's rather (in her own words) impulsive.

And of course, I'm not very easygoing or accommodating either. So, there were bound to be conflicts.

Why God why? Why can't adulting be easier?

Just days ago I was looking forward to spending the rest of my life with the woman of my dreams.

Today, we were arguing about the most cliché of things - from who to invite to the wedding to agreeing on the right venue, caterer, and decorator.

"I'm telling you, Abhay. Red and black for the engagement and peach and gold for the wedding."

And it's not like I could share my feelings with my parents either. They were always keen on seeing me get married and after they met Kaavya, they were happier than I'd seen them in years.

She was like the daughter they never had.

"Babe, I too want a dream wedding. But I also don't want to spend all my savings on a grand wedding party," I said shakily.

"I'm in my 30s and I definitely want to start being prudent about money, especially now that I'm getting married and taking on new responsibilities."

"Am *I* the new responsibility? Is that what you think, Abhay? I can't believe you're making me sound like some liability."

"Oh no. That's not what I meant. I just mean the more I save, the more we'll be able to spend in the future."

"You know me by now. I don't think about the future like that."

"Yeah, but that's exactly what we should start doing now. Thinking ahead!"

I tried to defend myself, but as is the case in most fights, it's a clash of egos, not facts.

"Who knows about the future, Abhay? What if I'm dead in 5 years? Take my mistress for a trip across Europe," said Kaavya mockingly.

Now what could I have said to that? At this point, it's never about who's right or wrong. It's just about not giving in to the other's whims.

Being in our 30s, we were both strong, opinionated people who didn't want to budge from our respective stands.

Therefore, what followed over the next few weeks were more such fights and disagreements.

I'm not saying there weren't fun and happy moments.

We'd still send surprise deliveries to each other's homes, and sometimes even show up ourselves.

I even took salsa classes with Kaavya because she thought it'd be fun (it was highly traumatic for me, to say the least).

We'd post selfies on social media proclaiming our love for one another (apparently the highest form of PDA in these times).

Our little getaways, where we shacked up and fooled around, also continued. We'd tell our parents we're going to "collect our outfits".

And we did collect outfits, *off* each other. So technically we weren't lying.

Although these moments seemed few and far between. A large part of our courtship was spent trying to bring each other on the same page.

Was this still the right decision for us? Doubts had started to creep in again. But we accepted this as a byproduct of the 'coupling' process and tried our best to focus only on the positives.

It was hard but I think we were doing fine, until that fateful morning when I *called off* the wedding.

CHAPTER 10

AU REVOIR, MA CHÉRIE

I'd like to believe I'm a patient guy, but what happened on February 14th was even beyond me. There was a different kind of performance pressure that day (no, not what you're thinking).

Kaavya called me and sounded elated on the phone. "Happy Valentine's Day, my love. I'm *so* happy today. You won't believe what happened."

Did she get the outfit of her choice in her size? Or did the band she wanted become available?

Of course, I kept my thoughts to myself and replied with the same enthusiasm, "Happy Valentine's Day, babe. You sound very excited. What's up?"

"You remember that project I'd applied for in October? The one in Paris that I was extremely keen on getting?"

"Yes!"

“I got selected! They’ve only picked 3 candidates from Asia and I’m one of them. Can you believe it?”

“Oh my God, that's wonderful, babe. I know you worked really hard on that one. Congratulations!”

“You can’t just congratulate me on the phone. We need to meet *now*!”

“Sure, I’ll pick you up in 30 minutes.”

“No, just come over. No one’s home anyway. I’ve also called for fresh strawberries and wine for you.”

Things were finally looking up.

I reached Kaavya’s home and we did what couples are expected to do in their courtship.

It was as if nothing was wrong. At that moment, none of the fights and disagreements mattered. All my doubts and worries instantly dissipated.

Somehow that always happened when I was with Kaavya. There was something truly magical about this girl.

I was standing in front of Kaavya’s mirror, stroking my hair with my fingers when she said, “Abhay, there’s something I need to tell you.”

I looked at her and said in a French accent, “Honeymoon in Paree, ma chérie?”

“About that…uhh...you know that the project is for 2 weeks, right?”

She continued, “It starts on March 4th.”

"Damn! That coincides with our wedding dates. What will you tell them?"

There was a long pause.

"Kaavya, you *will* tell them you can't make it for this one, right?"

There was an awkward silence, again.

"Abhay, listen. It's just that…I told them…," Kaavya murmured.

"You've already accepted it. Haven't you?"

"Abhay, you know how hard I worked for this," Kaavya said in a shrill voice.

"I've waited for a project like this all my life. It'll open up so many avenues for me."

Was *this* the real intercourse I was here for? I almost felt exploited.

"And what about our *dream* wedding? Is that not important anymore?" I asked loudly.

"No need to get sarcastic. We can figure this out together."

"How, Kaavya? How can we figure this out? This isn't one of your decisions you can make instinctively."

"Can we not move our wedding by a couple of days?"

"Move it by a couple of days? Everything is booked. Invitations have been sent. We can't do that!" I said firmly.

"You don't have to shout."

"I'm not shouting, Kaavya. Just tell me what you've finally decided to do."

"I told you. I'm not saying no to the project. We'll just have to figure out a way. Okay?"

"No! I've had enough. This definitely doesn't work for me. You rushed me into getting married and now you want to move the date. I'm not okay with this."

"You're being too unreasonable, Abhay. I would never get in the way of your work."

"Kaavya, this isn't one of your trips to Jordan that can be moved at your convenience. I'm not letting this happen."

"What do you mean, Abhay?"

"I mean I'm calling it off, Kaavya. There will be NO wedding!"

CHAPTER 11

HAPPILY NEVER AFTER

A couple of days went by without any communication.

We didn't want to tell our parents, but they had to get involved eventually.

Although their intervention didn't help either.

Kaavya was hell-bent on going to Paris and I was adamant about not moving the wedding dates.

While everyone close to me tried to pacify me and encouraged me to be more open-minded, I was not interested in compromising this time around.

Instead, I was hit by a series of existential questions on whether I even wanted to get married. Or was this just a grand facade that I was putting up?

I was not willing to budge, but I definitely wanted to sort things out.

It was Kaavya, for heaven's sake. The woman whom I was head over heels in love with and who finally made me want to settle down.

But she was being so nonchalant about this. Was this a one-sided affair? Why didn't she seem to care? Could I have been *this* wrong in reading a person?

I had to get answers!

Oh, and let's not forget there was also added pressure from the families.

But I'd like to believe that wasn't the reason I wanted to patch things up.

I had to speak to her at least once. This definitely couldn't be the end.

While I was thinking of an apt way to approach Kaavya, I got a message from an unknown number.

"Hey Abhay, this is Tanvi. We met at Mohit's party. Not sure if you know but Kaavya's leaving for Paris by the 8:30 FlyerFrance flight tonight. She was super upset after your fight & preponed her trip to avoid any drama. You guys should speak once. If I were her, I would've never ditched you. You're quite the catch!"

Was this so-called friend trying to hit on me or genuinely help?

Either way, there was no time to waste.

As I read the message, I was both surprised and furious.

Surprised because Kaavya was leaving in a couple of hours, and I had hardly any time left to even see her, let alone speak to her.

However, I was also furious because here I was trying to make things work, while she was planning to leave for Paris to have a gala time without paying any heed to our situation.

I really didn't know what to do. So I decided to do what I do best - THINK.

I needed some me-time and a clear mind to decide what needed to be done. I knew no one else but I could help me out here.

So, I locked my room, sat in a quiet corner, and put on my earphones.

I'm pretty sure my parents thought I was doing something else behind those closed doors.

While listening to meditative music and relying on my instincts to guide me, I just knew what I had to do.

Although it would be very unlike me to do what I was planning on doing. But love makes you do crazy things, doesn't it?

I decided to channel my inner Hindi film hero and confront my lady love AT THE AIRPORT!

Of course, I loved Kaavya, I loved her very much. And I definitely wanted to marry her and only her.

I was just really mad at her for not wanting to resolve the fight before leaving.

Was I willing to postpone the marriage if need be? Hell, yes!

I was just shocked to know she didn't care about it as much as I did.

But now was not the time to bring in my ego. I had to speak to her right away!

It was already 6:00 PM and I had no time to deliberate or even change my clothes.

I took the car keys and passport and rushed to the airport. I tried calling Kaavya from the way, but her phone wasn't reachable.

Was I too late? I hope she wasn't already on the flight. I drove like a maniac (not proud of it) and was at the airport in 30 minutes flat.

I knew I wasn't going to be allowed inside the airport so I booked the cheapest international flight I could find only to be able to enter.

Apparently, I was going to Nepal with no luggage or cash.

Kaavya's phone was still unreachable, so I literally would have to go through security and immigration only to somehow bump into her on the way.

While I was trotting towards the security checkpoint, I saw Kaavya at a distance. I couldn't believe that I was able to spot her from among hundreds of people at the airport.

But then again, I was much in love so maybe this was the lover's sixth sense after all (cheesy much?).

"Kaavyaaaaaaa," I shouted.

I did get a fair share of stares, but I couldn't care less.

She saw me too from afar and shook her head in amazement.

We literally ran towards each other.

"Abhay, what are you doing here?" she asked while giving me a tight hug.

At that moment, all my anger melted away.

"Well, I couldn't let you go. I really love you."

"I really love you too. I definitely didn't want to leave either without you being on board with the Paris idea."

"Yeah, right," I said sarcastically.

"See, you *still* don't trust me."

"No, no. I do. And it's fine. We can move the wedding. You go and have fun in Paris."

"Breaking news, baby. I'm not going to Paris!"

Kaavya continued, "I thought about how we left things and I felt horrible. Yes, this project is very important to me, but *you* are even more important."

"What? I…I don't understand," the excitement in my voice was evident.

"I told Tanvi to message you, only to know how you truly feel about me going. I'd declined the offer last night itself. I'm not going to Paris."

"But if you're not going, why are you at the airport?" I asked with a puzzled expression on my face.

"I was really missing you, but I didn't know how long it would take for us to be normal again. So I'm going to Goa for the weekend to just relax and destress."

"Classic Kaavya," I thought.

She continued, "I was sure you'd call or message after hearing about my fake trip. But I can't believe you came all the way to show how much you support my decision. I'm the luckiest girl on the planet."

I didn't explicitly agree with her, but in my head, I was nodding vigorously.

"So now what?" I asked.

"I don't know. Mmm…why don't you come along?"

"Really? I don't even have my clothes."

"That's okay. We'd hardly be needing them anyway," she winked.

I turned red yet again (this girl really knows how to make me blush).

"Uh, I guess I could go. It should be fun."

"Oh, it will be. I promise. Come, let's get you your ticket."

It was this very quality about Kaavya that I'd been attracted to - the fact that she could live in the moment, without worrying about the future.

I returned my fake ticket to Nepal and got a real one to Goa.

As was predicted, the trip was a lot of fun. The beaches, the shacks, the cocktails, and of course, the making out.

I'm just glad I hadn't planned a Bachelor Party; it couldn't have been better than *this*.

We got back in two days, and it was like nothing ever happened. The wedding preparations were in full swing, and everyone (including myself) was over the moon.

Kaavya and I spoke about what had happened and if we should have dealt with the situation differently.

I believe, as cliché as it may sound, communication is the key to every successful relationship.

And not just any communication; respectful communication that comes from a place of genuine understanding and empathy, while keeping egos aside (easier said than done).

Anyway, back to the wedding - everything that had happened was behind us, and we were all looking forward to the grand celebration.

We wanted to keep it a 'simple' affair, so we had 3 functions with *only* 700 guests.

Don't even get me started - 600 of those were Mr. Singhania's business colleagues, and we had to drop the idea of a destination wedding just to accommodate them.

Kaavya was more upset about that than me, so I didn't bring it up again.

Despite that, the wedding functions went off really well and quite frankly, I don't remember most of them.

However, I do remember having a *lot* of fun.

A day before the functions were to start, my brother-in-law gave me the best advice ever.

He said, "Abhay, there are going to be too many things going on at the wedding. A few things will go as planned while others will not. So don't worry about making everyone happy or everything perfect. It is your week. Just have a blast and enjoy your own wedding!"

This was probably the only sound advice my brother-in-law ever gave me.

Kaavya and I actually did end up having a ball at our wedding.

CHAPTER 12
BELLED THE CAT

Did you know that no Indian engagement party is complete without an old aunty doing a shimmy to an '80s number and an estranged uncle swearing loudly after a couple of dozen drinks?

My wedding was no different. The first function was the engagement party.

The theme was black and red, but most people seemed to think the dress code was optional. They instead chose to wear their finest robes (or so they thought).

Kaavya was wearing a shimmering red gown, while I was in a classic black tuxedo.

At the risk of sounding immodest, we looked great!

Everyone said, "What a good-looking couple!"

Okay, maybe not everyone but a few people did say that.

That night was all about drinking and dancing, and of course, the rings were also exchanged at some point.

I recall everyone around me was high (and I don't mean high on life). We all danced till the wee hours of the night, and I definitely didn't want this jamboree to end.

Kaavya and I were thrilled for obvious reasons, but it was nice to see how loud Hindi music combined with cocktails and kebabs made the vibe spirited (quite literally) for everyone in attendance.

As is usual for an engagement function, there was an ultimate dance-off between the friends and relatives of both sides.

Don't get me started on the rather suggestive performance by my uncle, slithering on the dance floor like a snake, with a strange lady (not his wife) taming him as his snake charmer.

It became the highlight of the night and possibly scarred me for life (I need to ensure the videographer deletes that footage).

The morning after was a blur. I'm so glad that we had the next function at noon so I could somewhat bring myself back to my senses.

This was our Mehendi and Sangeet ceremony. We decided to have a combined function so both sides of the family could partake in the celebration.

It also helps split the costs (not complaining about that either).

In my mind, this is practically a bonus function that's added as a filler between the engagement and wedding as a supporting act.

Although I sincerely hope the clothes few of the girls were wearing that day were more ‘supportive’.

Let’s just say there were a few malfunctions, but none of the guests complained.

Kaavya wore a flowing yellow pleated ghagra skirt and combined it with a green scarf. The floral print on her attire was so intricate, and may I add she looked divine.

I too had matched my colours to her outfit and wore a yellow kurta-pyjama with a green Indian waistcoat. I too looked…well…divine.

What a match, you’d say.

The function was outdoor and the decor was very earthy - there were traditional divans for seating, colourful drapes with ‘Jaipuri’ patterns, and fragrant floral arrangements with ‘mogras’ and marigolds.

Kaayva was seated in a corner with a few friends, getting henna put on her hands and feet.

The rest of us were enjoying Indian delicacies including chaat papri and dal-naan, as beautiful, foot-tapping folk music filled the air.

Every now and then I could hear Kaavya’s boisterous friends giggling and running around as if they were on a sugar high (I’m sure it was something else, though).

On occasion, I too was dragged to the dance floor by them, only to find my way back to the food counters as quickly as I could.

I swear I could’ve punched somebody if they called me ‘Jiju’ one more time.

And then came THE day (no, I won’t call it the “D” day, yet).

The day when a couple learns to sleep with their eyes open, with plastic smiles pasted on their faces the entire day.

Kaavya wanted a daytime wedding. I, on the other hand, just wanted *a* wedding.

I didn’t really have a point of view as long as I was the center of attention (okay, at least one of the two).

But it turned out to be a good idea after all. For one, the pictures came out stunning.

And more importantly, we got to enjoy the entire day instead of cramming everything in one evening and staying up for unearthly hours, waiting for the rituals to get done with.

What I didn’t anticipate, though, is how hot it could get given I was wearing what felt like seven layers of clothing.

But somehow, I managed to survive.

As is customary for the groom, I entered with a grand celebratory procession, riding a royal chariot and surrounded by my ‘battalion’.

I was wearing an ivory-white sherwani with pastel pink embroidery and a matching scarf and turban.

Everyone was rejoicing to the fanfare of the wedding band as we slowly made our way to the lawns where the function was to take place.

I received a warm welcome from Kaavya's parents, cousins, and friends with a traditional tilak ceremony (where the groom's forehead is anointed with sacred vermillion) and was eventually made to sit on a decorated throne-like chair.

I looked around, hoping for people to gaze at me in awe, maybe even clap when I sat down.

But all I could see were unfamiliar faces stuffing their faces with tikkas and other appetisers.

Moments after I was seated, I could hear the bridal entry music playing at a distance.

I knew it was time.

Nothing else mattered to me at that point. Not the lack of food, the scorching sun, or the absolutely unbreathable clothing.

Okay, maybe a little.

From a distance, I saw Kaavya entering. And my world just stopped.

She was looking like a floating angel. Partly also because she walked through a dense artificial fog as she entered.

I couldn't take my eyes off her as I naturally gravitated towards my to-be wife. We both looked at each other teary-eyed, feeling the gush of emotions that led to this epic finale, for this moment had finally come.

I took her hand and we walked onto the stage where the ceremonies were to take place.

We exchanged garlands and met the guests (most of whom didn't seem to recognize me and vice-versa). I was just glad to receive the gift envelopes they'd brought along.

Finally, we made our way to the 'mandap' where we walked around the holy fire seven times while making the promise to always love and respect each other.

Don't ask me to explain any of these vows. I was barely listening to them myself.

At last, it was done. We were finally married!

More importantly, *I* was finally married (no, it's not the same thing).

We took the blessings of the elders, and it was time for Kaavya's 'vidaai' - the final event that marks the completion of the wedding.

It's usually an emotional time for the bride and her family as she formally bids adieu to them.

However, neither Kaavya nor her parents seemed emotional.

Let alone being teary-eyed, they were chatting and cracking jokes as Kaavya walked outside the venue towards the car.

Not that I wanted her to cry, but a few tears wouldn't have hurt anyone.

If it counts, I was probably more emotional than she and her family combined.

Anyway, it was a wrap! We were finally united, and we couldn't be happier.

As we were about to sit in the car, someone standing at the back shouted, "Please make way for *Mrs. and Mr. Mathur*."

WAIT…WHO?!?!

CHAPTER 13

MRS. AND MR. MATHUR

"Come out right now! You've been in the bathroom forever."

"Please decrease the cooling of the air conditioner."

"How could your mom say that to me?"

"I don't think you should make pizzas at home again."

"Why are you on your phone all the time?"

You know when you grow up watching Hindi cinema where the couple ends up living "happily ever after", you have a certain perception about how life would be after you get married.

You believe that life would be all fun and games, song and dance.

Even when there are fights, they'll be cute and harmless, and eventually, you'll make up and go prancing in the rain, hand in hand.

Let me tell you, that doesn't happen. I mean, I didn't expect life to be like a rom-com movie. But still, you have *no* idea what's in store for you.

And mind you, you have to experience it for yourself. No one else's advice - good or bad - would work here.

Don't get me wrong. I don't think there's anything wrong with marriage.

I'm just saying you need to know *exactly* what you're getting into, but the irony is you will only know that only once you're in it.

Kaavya and I were very much in love when we got married, and we still are.

But courting someone is very different from living with that person.

There are a lot of ingredients that go into making this dish called 'marriage'.

And it's not just about adding the right stuff in; it's also about getting them in the right proportion, blending them together well, and giving the dish its appropriate preparation time (was I a chef in another life?).

To add to that, this so-called recipe for a happy marriage isn't always the same; it's ever-changing.

Yes, boys and girls. Welcome to adulting!

I don't claim to be an expert on the matter but after having met so many wonderful women in my life, I can tell you a few of the do's and don'ts of finding the right partner and creating a beautiful life together.

I'll break my 'pearls of wisdom' into 3 phases of pursuit - pre, during, and post.

In the 'pre' phase, as I'd mentioned before, you have to (cannot stress enough on have to) make sure you're taking this call by yourself. That means no societal obligations, no peer pressure, and definitely no parents telling you who you should be with.

It's very difficult, but equally important, to listen to your inner voice and find the person who would be right for *you*.

I may choose to have a list of prerequisites but it's important to know what I truly want from my partner and what I can give them in return.

It's important to drop those unrealistic expectations and find someone who has the same core as you - the same intrinsic values and outlook in life.

The superficial stuff will soon fade away, but your gut will never misguide you. So douse all that excess noise and listen to that inner voice that has always told you what's right for you.

Of course, you do have permission to talk to your to-be partner and reaffirm your feelings. Communication, as I've said before, is the key to any happy relationship.

The next phase, however, is exceptionally tricky. It's the 'during' phase.

After you've decided who to settle down with, it's important to discuss what your life together is going to be like.

I know life is unpredictable, and more often than not things will go awry even if you plan.

But it's still essential to get each other's perspectives on things that matter to you, especially life goals - marriage, kids, and money.

Might I add, have as many fights as possible (yes, you read that right).

As counterintuitive as it may sound, it's critical to know how badly you want to be with a person after having the ugliest of fights with them.

It's also a litmus test for how willing each one is to take that first step, keep their ego aside and resolve the fight.

In my humble opinion, this is *the* toughest phase and also the most imperative one.

wasteIt's okay to even extend the courtship period to explore each other's truest selves and reveal traits that wouldn't have been as obvious in the 'fun and games' dating phase.

If you both cross this phase successfully and with dignity, give yourselves a *huge* pat on the back. I'd say this love is one for keeps.

So, go ahead.

Make that commitment.

Take the plunge.

And begin your happily never after…I mean ever after.

If you've made it this far, my heartfelt congratulations to you.

Now that you're officially bound for all eternity (I know it sounds scary), let things flow.

And if you think the worst is over, you're going to be not-so-pleasantly surprised. The disagreements, fights, and arguments will continue, only the themes will change.

From not flushing the toilet properly to the temperature of the air conditioner at night, there's never going to be an end to this.

But maybe that's what makes it so exciting and dynamic. Otherwise, life would be so mundane.

Oh, but we're not done yet. This brings us to our last and final 'post' phase.

It's possible that over time you will get busy with your own lives - your individual career paths and personal aspirations.

As a result, that spark between you might also start to fade.

But don't *ever* let it burn out completely.

Find interesting things to do together. You already know each other's preferences (and weak spots), so take time out to spend with each other.

Be it date nights, movie marathons, make-out sessions, or even salsa classes, make them happen.

And it's not just about the fun stuff. There are going to be real ups and downs as well.

Be there for each other. It won't be easy, and it won't always be possible to do the right thing but try and have each other's back.

I know it's easier said than done, but support each other, find solutions together, and above all, love each other unabashedly.

At the cost of sounding philosophical, when you vibrate at the frequency of love, you won't just attract more of that in your life, but you'll also become a better version of yourself.

So go ahead, become a fully charged vibrator (pun intended).

CHAPTER 14

AWW, MY BABY!

Enough said. Let's address the elephant in the room, shall we - should one get married?

Well, there's no other way of saying this - it is after all an individual's choice.

For me personally, marriage has been like a roller coaster ride. You feel the adrenaline rush sometimes, and at times, you feel like throwing up.

There are times when you can't do without them, and others when you can't do with them.

But is it worth it? Well, totally!

Having someone to love and someone who loves you back is a feeling that can't be described in words.

And the best part is that if you've picked up the cues correctly and settled with the 'right' person - right for you of course -

you'd realize that this relationship came to you in the most unexpected ways.

What's more important is that you find yourself caring for that person without even trying.

You see beauty in their imperfections and they accept you for all your flaws. There are absolutely no judgements or guards around them.

You can croak in your awful voice, you can gyrate to your favourite cabaret number, and you can crack the most hideous of jokes.

You can cry, you can love, you can fight, you can annoy (maybe not too much). You can just *be!*

There's pure, unconditional, unabashed love. You're grateful for them and can't believe that you've been this lucky to have found them.

You'll love them, hate them, and even be possessive about them, but you will want to thank the universe every single day for bringing them into your life.

Okay, at least on most days you will. But that's not bad either.

And just like that, these moments will turn into days, days to weeks, and weeks to months.

Guess what? Today happens to be our first wedding anniversary. Yes, an entire year has passed just like that.

I decided to surprise Kaavya with a trip to the Maldives and this was without a doubt the best decision I could've made.

The cool breeze, white sands, and emerald-green water would make for the most romantic setting to mark the end of our first year of togetherness.

I booked one of the fanciest properties, and it was an adult-only one. This was to ensure we were away from all the crying babies and yelling parents.

Don't get me wrong. I have nothing against babies or their delightful shrieks. It's just not something I wanted to experience on my holiday.

Our resort mostly had newly married couples on their honeymoon, who stayed indoors for the most part of their trip for obvious reasons (what a waste!).

We, on the other hand, thoroughly enjoyed the property and all its amenities as well.

The first 2 days were in a beach villa, where we would literally run up to the beach every couple of hours only to be mesmerized by the clear waters and white sands.

I felt like I was in heaven. What could be better than *this*?

Well, our very next destination. It was even more breathtaking.

We spent the next 3 days of our trip at the water villa. Oh, man! I could live there forever. And I'm not even a water person.

The room literally opened to the sea and we could see stingrays and baby sharks swimming from under our feet as we sat out on the sun deck.

Although I'm sounding brave right now, I was quite petrified by the thought of sharks swimming near my feet. You can't blame me after seeing the kind of scary shark movies we've grown up with.

At one point, Kaavya had a hearty laugh when I literally jumped at the sight of a crab sitting between us. I know you won't believe this, but it was looking right at me with its big beady eyes.

Kaavya, on the other hand, was unruffled by its presence and gently pushed the crab back into the water with her bare hands.

One afternoon, we were strolling in the resort when Kaavya came across a large, colourful booth.

"Did you know we can do scuba dives here, Abby? Let's go!"

"Uhh, sure, Kaav."

Yes, we've got nicknames for each other now if you noticed.

We were #Abby&Kaav.

I was so not looking forward to the dive as I'd had my share of encounters with sea creatures.

I would've even gotten out of it if it wasn't for the scuba instructor's snide remark, "Last month I trained a 10-year-old kid. I'm sure he can give you company underwater, sir."

Both Kaavya and he laughed, and I wasn't going to let him get away with that.

So I had to fake being okay with marine life lest Kaavya thought I was a weakling.

I took a deep breath and started with the pre-dive training. The fear was real.

“You don’t have to do this, babe,” said Kaavya while emerging from the water like a mermaid.

“No, no. I’m fine. I want to do this, Kaav,” I said gasping for air.

The next 20 minutes or so were terrifying and I was sure I was about to drown.

But once we were in the water and I’d mastered the art of breathing through my mouth, I was quite at ease. So much so that the scuba dive turned out to be the highlight of our trip.

“I’m so proud of you, Abby.”

“Thanks, Kaav. I’m proud of me too,” I said valiantly.

I actually was proud of myself and at that moment, nothing seemed impossible!

It was the last evening of our perfect holiday. I was enjoying my beer while lazing in the sun when suddenly I was disturbed by a familiar voice.

“Abby, come quick. I’ve got to show you something.”

Kaavya pulled me by my arm, and I almost dropped the bottle from my hand.

“This better be worth it, Kaav.”

“Look, right there,” said Kaavya pointing at the sea.

“What is it, love?”

“Can you not see, Abby? Right over there.”

I squinted my eyes to see what appeared to be three grey blobs moving in unison.

"Oh, what are those? Fish?"

"Well, of course, they're dolphins silly. But there's something special about them."

"Umm, they're swimming in a group of three?"

"Pod, Abby. A group of dolphins is a pod. But they're not just any three dolphins. It's a *family*."

Kaavya continued, "Look, there's the mama and papa dolphin, and right between them is their little baby dolphin."

"Ah, that is cute."

"I know, right? They're taking such good care of their little one."

I stood there for a couple more seconds out of courtesy and after having realized I didn't have much to say, I wore my sunglasses and started turning back to return to my spot.

Ah, the divine comfort of lying on my beach bed without a worry in the world, with just the calming breeze and the soothing waves keeping me company.

"I'm sure I'd be a protective mother as well."

Kaavya's voice pierced straight through my heart.

Is she *kidding* me? Pun intended.

I stood there frozen, almost trembling. "Mother?" I retorted.

The pleasantness of the Maldives dissipated rather quickly, and I suddenly imagined myself in a tiny room crammed with babies, crying at the loudest decibel.

Who knew 3 dolphins would play *such* an integral role in my life?

I shut my eyes tightly to escape the thought, but there was no escaping. My mind, which was filled with soft nature-esque sounds, was suddenly clouded with deafening cries.

I'd barely come to terms with the fact that I'd been married. I definitely wasn't ready to become a dad yet.

And where was this thought even coming from? Do I not get a say here? We'd never spoken about this. Ever!

Kaavya tapped on my shoulder and said with a hint of disgust in her voice, "Relax. I'm not asking for this to happen tomorrow."

"But it will happen *someday*."

Can someone please hit the pause button on my life? Or on this woman?

How could I have a kid? I still *am* one.

All my endeavours to live in the moment floated away with those dolphins. I almost considered swimming along with them far into the horizon.

That was the end of the trip for me. For the rest of my holiday, all I could think about was dearest little Abby Junior.

THE END